MARGO BOND COLLINS

Cover Art:
Select-O-Graphix

Publisher's Note:

This is a work of fiction. All names, characters, places, and events are the work of the author's imagination.

Any resemblance to real persons, places, or events is coincidental.

Solstice Publishing - www.solsticepublishing.com

Waking Up Dead
by
Margo Collins

Chapter One

When I died, I expected to go to heaven.

Okay. Maybe hell. It's not like I was perfect or anything. But I was sort of hoping for heaven.

Instead, I went to Alabama.

Yeah. I know. It's weird.

I died in Dallas, my hometown. I was killed, actually. Murdered. I'll spare you the gruesome details. I don't like to remember them myself. Some jerk with a knife--and probably a Bad-Mommy complex. Believe me, if I knew where he was, I'd go haunt his ass.

At any rate, by the time death came, I was ready for it-- ready to stop hurting, ready to let go. I didn't even fight it.

And then I woke up dead in Alabama. Talk about pissed off.

You know, even reincarnation would have been fine with me--I could have started over, clean slate and all that. Human, cow, bug. Whatever. But no. I ended up haunting someplace I'd never even been.

That's not the way it's supposed to work, right? Ghosts are supposed to be the tortured spirits of those who cannot let go of their earthly existence. If they could be convinced to follow the light, they'd leave behind said earthly existence and quit scaring the bejesus out of the poor folks who run across them. That's what all those "ghost hunter" shows on television tell us.

Let me tell you something. The living don't know jack about the dead.

Not this dead chick, anyway.

It took me a while to figure out what had happened, of course. I came to, drifting along a downtown sidewalk in some strange little town. A full moon shone high above me, glinting off the windows of the closed stores. The only noise came from a little pub-like bar down a side street. I didn't know where I was or how I'd gotten there. What better cure for that than a stiff shot of something?

Next thing I knew, I was inside the bar. Like I was having those--whatchamacallits--those blackouts that people with multiple personalities claim to get. Fugues. I actually wondered for a minute if maybe that's what was going on.

Then I tried to order a drink. "Vodka martini, extra dirty. Lots of olives," I said when the bartender glanced my way.

The bartender ignored me. I tried again. The bartender walked away.

That's when I became Callie Taylor, Ghost Cliché.

I leaned over the dark oak bar and yelled after the bartender. "Hey! Down here! I want to order something." I got kind of a funny feeling in my stomach--like a muscle cramp or something. When I looked down, I realized I was standing in the middle of the bar, drink glasses and all. That concerned me, so I stepped right through it and to the other side.

I won't bore you with the rest of my moment of epiphany. Suffice to say, I figured out I could do lots of ghostly things--walk through walls, blow out candles just by passing over them, let people feel a chill when they moved through me. (I don't recommend it; it's kind of chilly on this side, too. Brrr.) But I can't do much of the old live-person stuff. I can't eat. I can't drink. I can sort of smell food and drink, and that's nice, but not nearly as nice as eating and drinking was. If I concentrate really hard, I can sometimes make things move just a little bit. Electronic stuff is easiest--I can make anything electric go haywire. But I couldn't talk to anyone.

I tried to. I used every ounce of concentration I had to make myself heard. I tried over and over again. I went all over town trying to get someone's attention.

Sometimes, some poor schmuck caught a glimpse of me. One guy just about peed himself when I showed up in a mirror behind him, and that made me feel bad. So I pretty much quit trying to do that after a while.

And of course I tried to leave. If I had to be a ghost, I at least wanted to see how my family was doing back in Dallas. Find some way to let Mom and Dad and my brother Craig know that I was okay, really.

To be entirely honest, I also kind of wanted to see my own funeral. See who was there. I especially wanted to know if Preston Davis had shown up at my funeral. Preston was a database administrator for a local hospital and had been my on-again-off-again boyfriend for a while. We'd met at my friend Amy's Halloween party and hit it off, but were both too busy to start up anything serious. At least that's what I told myself. Amy called him my "fuck buddy," and in my more honest moments, I had to admit to myself that there was little more to the relationship than that, no matter what I might have wished.

I wanted to know if he cried at my funeral and how--or if--he introduced himself to my family.

Yeah. Okay. So it's petty of me. So what? I'd had a rough week. Cut me some slack.

Anyway, I suspected that Preston sat with Amy and her husband Brian at the funeral. Amy, my best friend since college, would have been sobbing. Brian, the tall, kind, quiet man she'd married, would have been comforting her and occasionally wiping his own eyes with a tissue.

On the other hand, I imagined that Preston sat through the funeral stoically and then quietly left when the service was over.

Preston wasn't into big shows of emotion.

I'd spent the entire eight months of our relationship ignoring the fact that his lack of emotional affect bothered me. Now I found myself growing angry at his stoicism at my funeral.

Imaginary funeral, I reminded myself. *Imaginary stoicism. Imaginary Preston, for that matter.* I didn't have any idea what had really happened. Not that it mattered, at this point.

But there were other things I wanted to know, too. I wanted to know how long it had taken someone to go into my condo. I hoped not too long--I hoped someone had gotten to my cat Phoebe in time, that someone had fed her, given her water. That someone had adopted her and was feeding her right now.

I hoped Amy had taken Phoebe in. In fact, I was just going to assume that Amy had; it was easier on me.

But apparently I couldn't get to Dallas to check these things out. I couldn't even go outside of the city limits. I'd hit the edge of town, take one more step, and *pop!* I'd be right back in the middle of downtown. Don't get me wrong. Abramsville, Alabama is a lovely little town. Cute little downtown square with an ornate, nineteenth-century courthouse and shops selling knickknacks and jewelry and plaques with clever sayings on them. There's a college, a couple of bars, some beautiful old houses.

But it's not my town.

And it gets lonely, being the only ghost in town.

I know, I know. My best bet would have been to find other ghosts to hang out with. I tried it all. I hung out in hospitals, cemeteries, nursing homes, everywhere I could think of that other ghosts might congregate. I was even in the hospital emergency room a couple of times when other people died. All I saw was just a shimmer in the air above them, a wispy movement like light on fog. And then it was gone.

But as far as full-on, hanging-out-in-town ghosts? Nothing.

This went on for weeks. And in that time, you want to know what I learned about being dead?

It's boring.

Bo-Ring.

Until, that is, the night I saw some creep chop up Molly McClatchey.

Chapter Two

I had fallen into something of a routine by then. One of the things that all those ghost hunter shows get right is that some people seem to be more "sensitive" than others. Some people got all freaked out when I was around, even if they didn't know why. That's why I was able to make that one guy see me in the mirror.

So I started hanging out at the houses of people who were most emphatically *not* sensitive to my presence.

Just for the sense of companionship, mind you. I wasn't being all voyeuristic or anything. That would be creepy. I just missed being around normal people. Or any people at all, for that matter. I missed my life. I'd had a lot of friends. Every Sunday night Amy had hosted poker night. We took turns cooking--me, Amy, Brian, Lia, Elizabeth, Jim. Sometimes Preston even showed up, though he was more likely to order pizza for everyone if it was his turn to provide dinner.

The McClatcheys were the sort of couple who would have fit in perfectly with my friends in Dallas. I liked being around them. She taught art at the local college. He owned a musical-instrument repair shop. She was tiny, dark-skinned with long, black, curly hair and brown eyes. He was tall and thin with sandy brown hair. They were both in their late twenties. No kids, yet, but they were talking about it.

Yes. I heard them talking about wanting to have kids soon. So what? It wasn't gross or anything. On Thursdays, they watched the crime show that had been my favorite when I was alive. So around seven, after dinner, I drifted over and watched their television.

I can't help it if they had conversations while I was there.

And it's not like they were the only people whose homes I invaded. Haunted. Whatever. Mondays at the Stevenses' place. Tuesdays at the Andersens' home.

Wednesdays with the Smiths. And so on.

Like I said, I was bored.

Anyway.

This Thursday was different. Rick McClatchey had gone to some musician repairman conference. Molly had been at home by herself for several days, and I could tell she was ready for Rick to get home. She stood at the kitchen counter humming to herself as she chopped vegetables for a salad. Steaks sizzled on the small indoor grill. Potatoes wrapped in foil baked in the oven. Even I could smell the wonderful dinner she was preparing for Rick's return--another reason I liked to spend time at the McClatchey's: Molly's cooking always smelled great.

When the front door opened, I think Molly and I both expected it to be Rick.

"Hi, honey," she sang out from the kitchen.

No one answered, but Molly didn't seem worried.

"Dinner's almost ready," she said, loudly enough to be heard in the living room. "If you'll set the table, I'll get everything else together."

She didn't even turn around when the man walked into the kitchen. It's what Rick would have done, after all. And she was bent over the oven, pulling out the pan that held the baked potatoes.

I saw him, though. He wasn't Rick McClatchey. He wasn't anyone I'd ever seen before. He had dark hair--almost black--and pale blue eyes. Tiny pits covered his cheeks, like he'd had adolescent acne. He was shorter than Rick and more muscular. He wore regular clothes--Levi jeans and a black t-shirt--but he also wore black leather gloves and those little blue booties that doctors and nurses sometimes put on over their shoes.

And he had some sort of wire in his hands, the ends twisted into his grip.

I knew what was going to happen when I saw the wire. I started screaming. "Molly, no! Watch out!" I waved my arms over my head and screamed at the top of my lungs. I closed my eyes and concentrated on forcing my hands to make real contact with Molly, pushing as hard as I could with my hands and my mind, hoping to make her drop the pan and turn around.

It didn't do much good, though.

The pan of potatoes did slip out of Molly's hands and she danced backwards to avoid getting hit with the bouncing foil packages. But none of that stopped what was about to happen.

As Molly straightened up, the man slipped the wire over her head and twisted it around her neck. She struggled, but he pulled the garrote tighter and tighter.

I was screaming at the top of my ghostly voice, for all the good it did me. I moved up behind the man and beat at his back with closed fists--fists that slipped in and out of his back without ever making real contact. He shuddered a little-- clearly he was one of the very slightly sensitive ones--but he didn't loosen his hands.

I reached up and tried to grab the wire, tried to pull against the pressure he was exerting on the wire and it did loosen for an instant. But only for an instant. The living have more control over solid objects than the dead do. I never resented that fact more than at that moment.

But I kept trying. I kept trying as Molly's face turned purple, then blue, then black, kept trying even as she drooped in the man's grip.

Then he loosened the wire and it was too late. I watched that wispy, light-on-fog life force slip out of Molly and move on to wherever it is that other people go when they die. I was glad she didn't show up next to me as a full-blown ghost. At that moment, I wouldn't have wished my impotent half-existence on anyone.

I couldn't help thinking that if I'd been alive; I might have been able to save her.

If I could have cried real tears, I would have. As it was,

I was sobbing hoarsely and calling the man every dirty name I could think of.

I was still cursing as I followed him around the kitchen. First he opened the pantry and pulled out a box of Hefty garbage bags. Then he grabbed a knife out of the block on the counter. And finally, he picked up Molly's body and carried it to the bathroom.

What he did to her body was horrible.

I didn't want to stay. And I didn't want to watch.

But more than that, I didn't want this son of a bitch to get away with what he was doing.

He was meticulous; I have to grant him that. The garbage bags were for himself--he wore them to catch the blood splatter as he cut her up in the tub. He wore a dust mask, I guess to keep his DNA off of her. He traded his leather gloves for surgical gloves, making sure that everything he took off went into a pouch he wore on his belt.

I'd assumed that he would take Molly's body with him, but he didn't. He left her splayed out in pieces in the bathtub like some broken, disarticulated doll.

I'm no cop. Never was. When I was alive, I was a technical writer. I designed documents for one of the big phone companies--the sorts of instruction manuals that come with a CD and titles like *Easy Installation Instructions for Your New DSL.*

But I watched plenty of cop shows. Especially after I died. Not much else to do.

So when he started cleaning up, I waited for my chance. And eventually, he started to put the knife down into the tub next to Molly--apparently, he was planning to leave it behind. I wrapped my hands around his and twisted as hard as I could with both my hands and my mind, squinching closed my non-corporeal eyes and willing the knife to turn.

It did.

It slipped out of his hand and sliced cleanly through the glove he wore on his right hand and into the skin.

"Dammit." It was the first thing I'd heard him say. His voice was deep, almost gravelly. He grabbed a hand towel from the bar above the sink and held it to the wound.

So I tugged at the towel, pulling it toward the floor. It came loose from the wound for an instant before the man wrapped it more firmly around his hand.

But it was enough. A single, tiny drop of blood--his blood--had slipped out and landed on the side of the vanity.

He gathered up all the plastic bags, shoving them into yet another one. At the door, he traded his shoe-covering booties for another pair. Then he switched the surgical gloves out for the leather ones and went into the McClatchey's bedroom. He knew exactly what he was looking for, too--he went straight to Rick's dresser, opened a small wooden chest on top of it, and pulled out a tiny key. He gently closed the chest and dropped the key into his pocket.

He stopped at the door of the bathroom and stood back to survey the room. I stood in front of the vanity, willing his eyes to skip over that single drop of blood.

He tilted his head, his eyes narrowing as he stared at the vanity, stared at that blood drop. And then he shook his head and left.

It had worked. Hallelujah. Against all odds, I had kept him from seeing the evidence he'd left behind.

Now I just had to wait for Rick to get home.

Too bad I couldn't call 911 for him. I would have saved him this horror if I could have.

Poor Rick just about lost his mind when he came home and found Molly. It was horrible. I want to forget it almost as much as I want to forget my own death. Maybe even more.

The police took Rick away for questioning, of course. He had touched the body when he found it, so he had Molly's blood all over him.

It really was a mess. Even the poor policeman, who was first on the scene had to go outside for fresh air after just one look, I'm pretty sure I heard him retching in the bushes.

I considered following Rick to the police station, but I decided to wait for the Birmingham Crime Scene Unit to get to the house. Abramsville is a small town with a small police force. They're not really set up to deal with the blood evidence from gruesome murders.

Honestly, I was impressed. I wouldn't have been surprised if the small-town cops had arrested Rick immediately and called it a day.

But they didn't. They called Birmingham, and in the end, that was Rick's--and my--big lucky break.

I found out that night that crime scene stuff takes a lot longer than it looks like on TV. The police spent hours putting up crime scene tape, taking photos, examining the body, and removing the body. But eventually, a guy came in and started taking swabs of all the blood in the bathroom. He looked over everything pretty carefully, taking swabs from the tub, the floor, even around the toilet. And he looked at the vanity. But he missed the tiny blood drop the murderer had left behind. I stood beside it, jumping up and down on the balls of my feet, shouting "Here, over here!" But he wasn't one of the sensitive ones. He didn't sense a thing wrong.

So finally, I did the only thing I could think of.

I turned on the electric toothbrush.

Doesn't sound like much, does it?

Well, it was. I was already exhausted from all the energy I'd expended getting the murderer to leave the drop of blood behind in the first place and then keeping him from seeing it before he left.

But like I said, electronics are easiest of all, so I touched it and imagined twisting the wires as I sent energy coursing through them. Instantly, the toothbrush and its charger started jittering across the vanity. I gave them a little nudge with my finger and they headed toward the side of the vanity with the blood drop.

The CSU technician stopped in the doorway and turned around, frowning. He reached over and switched off the toothbrush. He gave the room a sweeping glance and turned to leave, still frowning.

I turned the toothbrush on again.

The technician froze in the doorway. He turned around slowly, staring at the toothbrush with narrowed eyes.

It continued buzzing its way across the counter.

The technician reached over and unplugged it. But this time he didn't leave. He stood staring at the toothbrush.

So I gathered up my last shred of energy and shoved the toothbrush as hard as I could. It skittered the last two inches to the edge of the counter and balanced there, just on the verge of falling off.

The technician stared at it intently.

And then he saw the blood.

I knew the moment he saw it, too. The suspicion disappeared from his face. He leaned in closer to the counter, zeroing in on the blood drop.

Almost absently, he used his gloved forefinger to push the toothbrush back to its place on the counter. Then he set his kit down on the floor, pulled out a swab, and swiped it through the blood.

Finally confident that Rick wouldn't go to prison for his wife's murder, I retreated, exhausted, to the living room.

*   *   *   *

Ghosts don't really sleep. This one doesn't, anyway. Never having met another ghost, I can't speak for anyone but myself. I do, however, just sort of drift. It's a little like daydreaming--I'm aware of what's going on around me, but I don't really pay attention to it. If I wanted to, I could spend days and days like that. In fact, sometimes I did.

This time I didn't seem to have a choice. I had probably expended too much of my spook energy--or whatever it is--keeping Rick out of trouble.

Or so I thought.

I think I drifted for about three days. In that time, I have a vague recollection of police officers moving through the house periodically. Crime scene techs vacuumed up everything that might be on the floors and took all the trash bins with them.

When I finally regained full consciousness, the house was empty. I realized that Rick had never come home.

That worried me.

So I put my hand on the television and concentrated until it came on, then worked at flipping through the channels until I found the Birmingham news station.

I didn't have to wait long. A gruesome murder like this one was big news, not only in Abramsville, but in all the nearby towns and cities. It might even hit the national news soon. A still photo of Rick flashed across the screen, then a picture of Molly, taken at her wedding. The photo receded to a corner of the screen, replaced by a moving image of Rick, in handcuffs, being shoved into a police car.

". . . Rick McClatchey, indicted today for the strangling murder of his wife, Molly McClatchey," the blonde newscaster was saying, "due to the presence of his DNA on the piano wire used to kill her."

I turned the television off. I didn't want to hear any more.

All my hard work, for nothing.

Had the crime lab even tested the blood drop from the real killer?

Apparently the evidence I had arranged wasn't going to be enough.

I know it wasn't my problem. Not really.

It's not like I'm some sort of guardian angel or anything. Ugh. Just the thought of all that responsibility gives me the creeps.

But Rick hadn't done it. Some other scumbag had. And that scumbag was walking around having a grand life while Rick was going to jail.

That just wasn't right.

I went back and forth, considering.

I wasn't sure what, if anything, I should do.

But the McClatcheys were the closest thing I had to friends in Abramsville.

Not that I could help. I could barely turn on a television.

Not alone, anyway.

In the end, I made up my mind.

I needed help.

Chapter Three

Like I said, I had taken to hanging out with people who weren't sensitive to my presence. But now I needed to find someone who *was* sensitive.

In fact, I needed someone who was more than just a little "sensitive." I needed someone I could talk to. If such a person even existed.

So I started looking.

Abramsville is a small town, but it still has roughly 15,000 people. Surely one of them had to be sensitive to ghosts. I didn't, however, consider how long it would take to test that many people. Or even just the adults.

So I started with the ones that I already knew had some sensitivity. I made my way to their houses, stood in front of them, waved my arms, jumped up and down, and screamed until I would have turned blue in the face if I'd been alive.

Some of them jumped a little, startled by something they almost saw out of the corners of their eyes. Several of them shivered and turned up the thermostat or wrapped themselves in sweaters.

And the guy who had seen me behind him in the mirror? This time he really did pee himself. Desperate as I was, I decided that he was too easily spooked to help me. What policeman was going to believe some pee-soaked lunatic who came in blathering about the evidence a ghost had told him about? He'd probably get arrested himself. Anyway, I had absolutely no assurance that he actually heard me when I said, "Please. You have to help me."

And to be honest, I have no idea what he saw. When I looked down at myself, I saw just me, wearing the clothes I'd worn the day I died. Black slacks, gray button-down shirt, black leather jacket, medium-heel black boots. Casual professional. When I'd managed to cast a reflection in the mirror, I'd still looked like me. Medium-toned skin, green eyes, dark wavy hair to my shoulders. A relatively attractive woman who could stand to lose five or ten pounds. Normal.

But for all I knew, when he saw me, I looked like I must have looked by the time I died. And from what I remember, that sight would be enough to make just about anyone soil himself.

I pretty quickly gave up on going door-to-door. I know the wheels of the legal system grind slowly, but I really didn't know how much time poor Rick McClatchey had. And time seemed to run differently for me now; I would go into my drifting phase and wake up to realize that days, not hours, had passed. So I began going to places where people congregated in large groups.

I started with churches. I figured, people in churches are believers, right? They've got to have some connection to the Great Hereafter.

Not a single one of them saw me.

Maybe the trouble was that I wasn't part of the Great Hereafter. I was just hanging out on the wrong side of the Right Here and Now.

I tried the college next. I did my little "Here I am, look at me now" song and dance right up in front of a whole classroom. One guy clearly saw me, but went scrabbling in his book bag for a bottle of prescription medicine. When I floated over to check it out, I saw that it was labeled "Haldol." Even I knew that that was some sort of anti-psychotic medication. Poor guy. I left that classroom immediately. Psychosis was even better than pee-soaked pants for demolishing credibility.

I finally found her at Wal-Mart, of all places. I had decided that in a town as small as Abramsville, just about everyone would eventually go to Wal-Mart. So there I stood in the entrance, just like the little old ladies who worked as greeters, spending hours on their feet saying "Welcome to Wal-Mart" to everyone who walked through the door.

I didn't say "Welcome to Wal-Mart." I didn't say anything, usually. I just stood in front of customers' shopping carts, hoping they would see me. For the most part, though, the few who paused did so because they needed to drop a purse into the cart, tell a child to catch up, adjust a strap on a sandal. Not because they saw me. Some of them walked right through me. Brrr. Some of the more sensitive among them skirted me without ever even knowing why. Until Ashara. She pushed her cart right up to me, within inches, and stood there for a second, staring straight into my eyes.

"Excuse me," she said. "I need to get through here."

I blinked. "You can see me?" I asked.

Her forehead wrinkled and she held her hands out in front of her, palms up. "Well, yeah." She shook her head.

I looked at her more closely. There didn't seem to be anything special about her--not metaphysically, anyway. Physically, she was beautiful. She was short, about 5'3", African-American, with huge brown eyes and clear, dark skin. Her hair, brown with red highlights, fell in tiny ringlets down past her shoulders. She wore blue jeans and a red t-shirt. I put her at about twenty-four or twenty–five, just a little younger than I had been when I died.

Watching me assess her, she took a deep breath. Her nostrils flared. She gripped the handlebar of her shopping cart more tightly. "If you're done staring, why don't you get out of my way before I run your white ass over," she said.

"Oh. Sorry," I said, so nonplussed that I actually moved out of the way.

"Bitch," I heard her mutter as she walked by.

This was not going as well as I might have hoped.

"Hey," I said, hurrying after her. "Wait up."

"I know you're not talking to me," she said. She stared straight ahead and pushed her cart down the middle of the aisle toward housewares.

"I am talking to you. Look. I know this is really weird, but I need your help."

"Well, I'm not talking to you. I don't know what your problem is, but you can take it somewhere else."

I wanted to reach out and grab her cart, to make her

stop and talk to me, but of course I couldn't. Which gave me an idea.

I scurried out in front of her, planting myself in her path.

"Move," she said.

"Not until you hear me out. Please?"

She moved her cart to the left. I stepped out to intercept her. She moved to the right. So did I.

"You got some kind of death wish or something?" she asked.

I laughed and shook my head. "If only you knew."

"I've got no time to talk to no crazy white lady in the Wal-Mart," she said. And she slammed into me with her shopping cart.

At least, that's what she planned to do.

The shopping cart, however, slid right through me. When it stopped, the basket had sliced cleanly through my midsection. The bottom rack merged with my ankles. From my perspective, it looked like two perfectly solid objects--me and the shopping cart--had melted together. I don't know what she saw.

Whatever it was, it wasn't good.

The woman's eyes widened, and then rolled up into her head as she slumped to the ground in a dead faint.

I bent down to try to wake her up, but no matter how hard I concentrated on making contact, I couldn't even touch her.

I hate being a ghost.

*   *   *   *

Luckily, there were other people in the store, and they could help her. Someone called the manager, and pretty soon there was a small crowd around her. She woke up blearily, looking around at all of the faces surrounding her.

"What happened?" the manager asked her as he helped her to her feet.

"There was this woman," she began, shaking her head.

Then she saw me, leaning in over all the other people around her--easy enough to do if you can float up three or four feet off the ground.

"That one," she said frantically, pointing at me. The people between us stared around at one another.

"Which one?" asked the manager. "What did she do?"

The woman pointed at me again. "That one. The white woman. In the black jacket."

Again, everyone looked around expectantly.

Finally, the manager placed his hand on her back and leaned in close to her. "Honey, there's no white woman in a black jacket here. Are you sure you're okay?"

The woman looked from him to me and back again. "You don't see her standing there."

He shook his head. "No. I don't. Is there anyone you want me to call for you?"

She stepped away from him. "No. No thanks. I'll be fine." She pulled her purse out of her basket and moved away, never taking her eyes off me or turning her back on me.

She hit the parking lot at a run. I moved right beside her, talking the whole time.

"Look," I said. "I'm not going to hurt you. I didn't mean to scare you. I just need help."

The woman was muttering under her breath, and after a minute, I realized that she was praying.

This was awful. I had absolutely no desire to terrify this poor woman, but she was the only person who had actually seen me in days of trying. And she could hear me, too. I couldn't let her go. I had to get her to listen to me.

So I followed her to her car. She ran as hard as she could, fumbling with the keys to the old Chevrolet. By the time she got into the car and slammed the door behind her, I had settled into the back seat.

She adjusted her rearview mirror, saw me in it, and screamed. Then she put her head down on her steering wheel and started sobbing.

"Hey," I said, reaching out toward her but unable to pat her on the shoulder. "Listen. Really. I mean it. I'm not going to hurt you."

"I just," she said, choking out words between sobs, "never thought that I'd get haunted at the Wal-Mart." The last word ended with a wail and another bout of sobbing.

"But you thought you might get haunted somewhere else?" I asked.

"Why won't y'all leave me alone?"

"Y'all? As in, more than one?"

She nodded, sniffling.

"What's your name?" I asked.

"Ashara."

"Okay, Ashara. So I'm not the first ghost you've met."

"No. You're just the first one who's talked to me in the Wal-Mart." She wiped the back of her hand across her eyes and turned to glare at me suspiciously. "Why you haunting the Wal-Mart, anyway?"

"I'm not haunting Wal-Mart," I said. "I was trying to find someone who could see me, who could hear me."

"Well, why don't you just go on back in there and find someone else?"

"Because I've been looking for days, and you're the only one I've found. And I'm running out of time."

"Looks to me like you already ran out of time, what with being dead and all," she said.

"Thanks for the reminder," I said dryly. "I'll tell you what. I'll make you a deal. If you'll listen to my story, listen to what I know and what I need help with, then I'll get out of the car and let you go if you decide you don't want to help me, okay?"

"Promise?" She stared at me, her eyes narrow.

"Promise. Cross my heart," I said, making the appropriate X over my chest. "Though I guess that the 'hope to die' bit doesn't really apply here," I added. That one got a snicker from Ashara.

"Okay, then," she said. "Talk."

"First you have to promise to seriously consider helping me."

She nodded. "Promise."

So I told her my story, all about Molly's death and Rick's arrest. About my determination to help Rick by finding the real killer. She stared at me intently the entire time, her eyes wide.

When I had finished, she lowered her eyes and took a deep breath to regroup.

Chapter Four

"You have got to be shittin' me," Ashara said.

"No. Really. That's how it happened. And I need someone to go to the police, to tell them what really happened. Rick can't go to prison for this. He didn't kill his wife. The police need to know that."

"And you think that I should just go walking on in there and tell the police that I got some new information about that white guy who killed his wife?"

"Well . . ." I paused for a moment, thinking it through. "Yeah, I guess," I said.

"And you think the cops are going to take me serious for even a minute?"

"They might," I said lamely.

Ashara shook her head. "No. I'll tell you what'll happen if I go in there. They're going to want to know how I know what I know. Then, when I tell them that some white lady ghost told me, they're going to kick me out on my ass."

"Then there's got to be some way to make them believe. Not in me. I don't care if they know about me. But maybe we can find some more evidence, something that will clear Rick."

Ashara shook her head. "Uh-uh. No way, no how. Whoever killed that lady might still be around. I'm not doing anything that might get his attention. You think someone like that's just gonna let me go digging around looking for evidence? Nope. Next thing you know, I'll be getting myself choked with some wire. No. Not happening."

My shoulders slumped in defeat. I sighed--or did the supernatural equivalent of it, anyway. It felt like sighing to me. "There's nothing I can do to get you to help?"

"Nope. Not a chance. Sorry, lady. Now I've got to go back into the Wal-Mart and get some light bulbs."

"Okay," I said. "Well, thanks for listening, anyway."

"Fine. Just get out of my car."

I did, and then watched her walk back into the store.

The only true sensitive I'd found in town, and she refused to help me. I stomped my foot on the ground and watched it sink several inches into the asphalt parking lot.

You know, it's not like what happened to me was the usual after-death thing--if that were the case, I guessed, there'd be ghosts all over the place. But there weren't any other ghosts anywhere in this town, as far as I could tell. And now the only person I could actually speak to had kicked me out of her car.

I've never really been the introspective type. But when a girl wakes up dead in Alabama, she's got to wonder why, at least a little bit. And I was beginning to really believe that I was somehow, for some reason, supposed to keep Rick McClatchey from going to prison for his wife's murder. This wasn't just a Good Samaritan moment, I thought. This was my whole reason for still being on this earthly plane.

And if I was right about that, then I didn't have to keep my promise to leave Ashara alone.

That's how I rationalized it to myself, anyway.

So by the time Ashara got back out to her car, Wal-Mart bag of light bulbs in hand, I was waiting for her in the passenger seat.

"You know," she said, as she got into the driver's seat and started the engine, "you being a liar about leaving me alone don't make me want to help you."

"But maybe you'll change your mind if I stick around long enough," I said.

She just rolled her eyes and pulled out of the parking lot.

We drove to a neighborhood on the north side of town where the houses were older, a little more run down. Ashara pulled up in front of one house with peeling white siding and a slightly sagging front porch. She walked through the front door and into the living room without knocking.

"Hey, Maw-Maw," she said, bending to kiss the old woman sitting in a recliner in front of the television. The furniture in the room was old, but well cared for. Handmade quilts covered the couch and the recliner. A rocking chair sat in another corner.

The old woman had a bun wound tight against the back of her head. Some wisps of gray hair floated around her face. She clutched a well-worn afghan around her and peered myopically around the room through glasses as thick as the bottoms of old-fashioned Coke bottles.

"I brought your light bulbs," Ashara said. "I'll go change that one in the kitchen right now." She moved through a doorway and out of sight.

Maw-Maw continued to stare around the room.

"Ashara, honey?" she called out, her voice trembling with age.

"Yes, Maw-Maw?" Ashara answered from the other room.

"Why you got a white lady haunt with you?" She pronounced the word more like "haint."

Ashara sighed and I could practically hear her eyes rolling. "I don't know, Maw-Maw. She just found me at the Wal-Mart and now she won't go away."

I stared at the old woman, my eyes huge.

"She tell you what she want?" Maw-Maw asked Ashara.

"Something about some white dude killed his wife."

"He didn't kill his wife," I said, loudly enough for Ashara to hear. "That's why I need your help."

"Well, if he didn't do it, who did?" Maw-Maw asked me.

"You can hear me?" I asked, stunned.

"Of course I can hear you," Maw-Maw said. "I need glasses, not a hearing aid." I stood in the doorway, unable to think of a single thing to say.

"Well," said Maw-Maw, "quit standing there with your mouth hanging open. You look a fool. You might as well come on in and set yourself down."

So I did. I moved over to the couch and sat down. That's one of the strange things about being dead but still hanging around--I can float or I can walk. And I can sit down, if I want to. I can also apparently stomp my foot right through the Wal-Mart parking lot if I get mad enough. But none of it's really conscious.

Maw-Maw peered at me through her thick glasses. I could hear Ashara in the kitchen, dragging a chair over and clambering up onto it, unscrewing the burned-out light bulb and putting in the new one.

"So," Maw-Maw said. "Why you haunting my granddaughter?"

"I'm not haunting her," I explained, leaning forward earnestly. "I just need her help. She's the only person who has actually seen me since I've been in Abramsville."

Maw-Maw's eyes narrowed. "You ain't from around here, are you?"

I sighed. "No. I'm from Dallas."

"So why you here?"

"I don't know. I died in Dallas. And then I just woke up dead. In Abramsville. I don't know why I'm here. I don't know how I got here. But I saw someone kill Molly McClatchey, and it wasn't her husband. But he's the one they arrested."

"She that girl got killed with a piano wire?" Maw-Maw asked.

"Yes."

"Mm-hmm." Maw-Maw nodded. "I saw that on the TV. They arrested him yesterday."

"And it don't have a damn thing to do with us," Ashara said from the kitchen doorway.

"You watch your mouth, child," Maw-Maw said.

"I just don't know who else to go to," I said.

"Hmm." Maw-Maw's eyes closed. Her head dropped to her chest and she began breathing deeply and regularly.

Is she asleep? I wondered.

"Okay, Maw-Maw," Ashara said, gently touching her grandmother on the shoulder. "I'm gonna go now. You need anything else before I leave?"

Maw-Maw's head snapped up--much more quickly than I would have expected from such an old woman. "You sit yourself down, Ashara Jones. You ain't going nowhere until you figure out what to do with this white ghost lady."

"Maw-Maw," Ashara whined.

"No, ma'am." Maw-Maw's voice was no longer trembling. In fact, it was practically strident. "You brought this dead white lady over to my house. So you can just sit yourself down next to her and listen to what I have to say."

Ashara sighed and sat down as far from me on the couch as she could possibly get. She crossed her arms over her chest and pressed her lips together.

"Now you listen to me, Ashara. God gave you a gift, one that you ain't never used before. And if God didn't want you to see no dead white ladies, you wouldn't. But you seen this one. And heard her, too. She's here asking for your help. And you are going to give it to her. You hear me?"

Ashara turned and glared at me. "Yeah."

"What did you just say to me, Ashara Marie Jones?"

"Yes, ma'am." Ashara sounded resigned.

"Good." Maw-Maw nodded to herself and wrapped her afghan around herself a little tighter. "Now you two girls get on out of here and figure out what you got to do next. My story's about to come on the TV and I don't want to miss any of it."

Ashara stood up and leaned over to kiss her grandmother on the cheek. "Bye, Maw-Maw."

Maw-Maw patted Ashara's hand. "Thank you, baby. You're a good girl."

I stood awkwardly by the door. "Thank you, ma'am," I finally said as Ashara brushed passed me without even glancing my direction.

Maw-Maw waved her hand without looking at me.

"Good-bye, ghost lady. Don't you go getting my Ashara in trouble."

How was I supposed to answer that? "Um. Okay. Bye," I finally said.

I followed Ashara out the door, barely managing to slide my ethereal butt into the passenger seat of her car before she pulled away from the curb, tires squealing.

"I don't have to help you just because my Maw-Maw says I do," she said.

"I know."

"I don't have to help you at all."

"I know," I said again.

"So why are you still in my car?" Her hands gripped the steering wheel tightly.

"Because you're going to help me."

"What makes you think that?"

"I saw the way you looked when your grandmother said you had a gift from God."

"So what?"

"You believe her. You believe you have a gift from God and if you don't help me, you'll feel guilty about it for the rest of your life."

"You believe I got a gift from God?"

"I don't know," I said.

"You believe God sent you to me?" She glanced at me out of the corner of her eye.

"I don't know what I believe," I said after a long, silent moment. "I mean, I used to believe in heaven. But what I got when I died was Alabama."

"Why do you want to help this guy stay out of jail so much?" she asked. "You think if you save this guy, you might get to go to heaven?"

I let the silence drag out on that one. Finally, I said, "Maybe. I don't know. But I do know that he didn't do it." I shrugged. "Isn't that reason enough?"

"I don't know," Ashara said. "People go to jail every

single day for things they didn't do. I can't save all of them."

No," I said, "but maybe you can save one."

Ashara sighed, her shoulders slumping. "Okay. Fine. What do you want me to do?"

Chapter Five

"I guess the first thing we should do is try to find some evidence that will exonerate Rick McClatchey," I said.

"And how are we supposed to do that?"

"Well, the only thing that I know was in his home was already collected by the police."

"That blood you told me about," Ashara said, nodding.

"Yeah. So I think that maybe the next place we should look is his shop."

"What shop?"

"His musical instrument repair shop. If his DNA is on it, that's probably where the killer got the piano wire."

"And how do you think we're going to get into that place?" Ashara was looking at me out of the corner of her eye again. Suspiciously.

"Well. I guess we'll have to go into the shop," I said slowly.

"Go into?"

"Yeah."

"You mean break into." Ashara pulled the car over to the curb and stopped it, then turned in the seat to face me full-on. "Do you know what the police do to black people they find breaking into stores?"

I didn't answer.

"They put them in jail and throw away the key. And that's if they're lucky. If they're not lucky, the police shoot them. On sight. And then claim that they were attacked."

"Oh, come on. It can't be that bad."

Ashara tilted her head, raised her eyebrows, and pursed her lips. "It's that bad. And you are not going to get my ass thrown in jail."

"Then we just won't get caught," I said decisively.

"Oh yeah? And how do you plan to make sure that don't happen?"

"I don't know yet. But I'll think of something."

"It looks all clear," I whispered, sliding back into the passenger seat--without ever opening the car door, of course.

"You don't have to whisper," Ashara said--though she, too, was whispering. "No one else can hear you."

We were parked about a block from the musical instrument repair shop, a small storefront in the downtown square. At 10:00 at night, everything was dark except for the bar a few blocks away. I had gone into the shop and looked things over. Nothing seemed out of place in any way, as far as I could tell. The front showroom was neat and orderly. The back room had several work benches with tools and instruments in various stages of disrepair scattered across them.

The shop had an alarm system, but it was electronic, so I had been able to disable it fairly easily.

Callie Taylor, Ghost Criminal.

I hoped I had done everything I could do without Ashara's help.

"Did you remember to bring gloves?" I asked her.

"Yeah. I got them in my pocket." She patted the side of her jacket.

"Good, then. Ready?" I asked her.

She took a deep breath. "Ready as I can be."

"Let's go, then" I said, slipping out of the car. Ashara's exit wasn't quite as silent as mine, since she had to open the car door to get out and then close it again behind her. But at least she didn't slam the door.

We strolled down the sidewalk and ducked into the alley behind McClatchey's shop. The back door was about halfway down the alley. A dumpster on one side of the door blocked the view of the door from the street.

Ashara reached out for the doorknob.

"Wait!" I said. "Gloves!"

"Oh, man," Ashara said. Her hands shook as she pulled the gloves out of her pocket and tugged them on.

"Okay. Now. Try the door," I said.

Ashara wiggled the knob. It moved easily. Then she pushed at the door. It didn't move. "Locked," she said. We both stared up at the key-hole to what was clearly a bolt lock about a foot higher than the doorknob.

"We're just going to have to pick the lock," I said, nodding emphatically.

"You know how to pick a lock?" Ashara asked.

"No. Do you?"

"What--you think all black chicks know how to pick locks?"

Ashara looked at the door, muttering to herself. I didn't catch much. Just something about "stupid." I decided to ignore it.

"Can't you do something all ghosty and shit and unlock it?" Ashara finally asked.

"What? You think all ghost chicks know how to pick locks?"

Ashara stared at me for a long moment, and then finally grinned. "Okay, okay. Fine. How do you think we can do this?"

I stared at the lock. "Wait here," I said. I moved through the door and to the other side. On this side, the bolt was a simple twist knob. It wasn't electric, so it was going to be harder, but maybe I could do it.

I took the ghostly equivalent of a deep breath and held on to the lock, twisting it with my hand, all the while picturing it open, imagining the bolt popping out of the socket in the door frame. Slowly, ever so slowly, the knob began to turn. After a few moments, I had to stop to take a break.

I popped just my head through the door into the alley. "It's working," I said triumphantly.

"God. Don't do that," Ashara said. "That's creepy, seeing just your head coming out that door. Damn, girl. Go back inside."

"I just thought you'd want to know," I said, the smile

dropping from my face. I moved back inside and went back to twisting the knob.

Finally, the bolt sprung back.

"Okay. It's open," I said, loudly enough so that Ashara could hear me from outside.

Ashara slowly turned the doorknob and pushed the door open. We both waited for a moment, listening for the sound of an alarm.

"I think we're okay," I finally said.

"So what are we looking for?" Ashara said, glancing around the workroom.

"I'm not exactly sure."

"Well, we don't have all night. I got to go to work tomorrow."

"Work?" I said. "Where do you work?"

"You don't gotta sound so surprised. I got a job. I work at the bank. Abramsville First National. I'm a teller at the drive-through window. So yeah, I gotta be at work tomorrow at seven-thirty."

"I wasn't surprised. Just curious--it's not like you said anything about it before.

"Fine," Ashara muttered. "So where should we start?"

"I guess with piano wires, since that's what that guy killed her with."

We began by searching the front of the store. Ashara had brought a tiny flashlight with her, the kind that attaches to key chains.

"Be careful with the light," I said. "We don't want anyone to see it from outside."

"I am being careful," she said. "What do piano wires look like?"

"I don't know. It was just a wire. He had it wrapped around his hands."

We moved to opposite sides of the store.

"So you saw him kill her?" Ashara asked.

"Mm-hmm. It was pretty awful."

"The news said he cut her up pretty bad." Ashara's voice was solemn.

"He did. Like a butcher. In the bathtub."

Ashara was silent for a moment. "How'd you die?" she asked quietly.

"Can we please just look for piano wires?" I snapped. I felt bad when Ashara didn't say anything, but I really didn't want to talk about my own murder. I wanted to focus on catching the man who had killed Molly McClatchey.

"Found some," Ashara finally said. She stood in front of a peg-board display. Coils of wire in plastic bags hung in rows, each labeled with a number--sizes, I guessed.

"These are in bags, though," I said doubtfully. "Maybe we ought to look in the back workroom, where the bags might have been opened."

I floated toward the workroom, Ashara behind me.

Just as I got to the doorway, I heard a sound coming from the alley. Then I saw the doorknob start to turn. I frantically searched my mind, but couldn't remember if Ashara had locked it behind us when we'd come in.

"Someone's here," I hissed. "Hide." I turned around and shooed my hands at Ashara, who stood frozen, eyes huge as she stared at me.

"Move!" I barked out. "He can't see me, but he can see you. Hide!"

Ashara spun around, took two or three steps, and ducked down behind the nearest large object--a display case holding a variety of musical instruments. She moved to the corner where the counter met the wall, where the shadows were darkest.

"Stay down," I said. "Don't move. Don't even breathe unless I tell you to."

I turned back around in time to see the door swing slowly open and a figure step slowly through the entrance.

"Oh my God," I said.

Ashara stared up at me from behind the counter, biting

her bottom lip worriedly.

"It's him," I whispered, even though I knew the man wasn't sensitive enough to hear me. "The one who killed Molly."

Ashara shrank down even further, squeezing her eyes shut.

The man moved into the workroom, looking around, letting his eyes adjust to the darkness.

A tiny whimper escaped Ashara, and the man froze, his eyes riveted toward the front of the store.

Chapter Six

I spun around in search of something to distract him. There. On the top of the front entrance to the store--one of those old-fashioned bells that rings every time someone comes in. I hastened to the front of the store, reached up, closed my eyes and focused on just barely, barely tapping it, as if a breeze had floated by. The man looked around again, searching for the source of the sound. I let him look for a moment before making the bell chime lightly again.

This time he found the sound. Moving to the front of the store, he examined the bell. Satisfied, he headed back toward the workroom. I stood in front of the counter, willing him not to see Ashara crouched in her dark corner.

He kept walking.

I let out a sigh of relief and followed him into the workroom.

He walked directly to one of the workbenches, shuffling through the pile of tools and parts that lay scattered across it. He picked something up and put it in his pocket. I couldn't tell what it was.

He moved to the door again and took a last look around. He nodded, apparently satisfied with something, then left. I heard him lock the door behind him.

"He's gone," I called out to Ashara. "You can come out now."

Ashara didn't answer.

I floated over the top of the counter and peered down at her. She was still huddled in the corner, arms wrapped around her knees and rocking back and forth.

"It's okay, Ashara. He's gone. You can come out now."

She shook her head back and forth several times. "It is not okay. That man is a murderer and he was in here with us. There is nothing okay about that."

"Come on," I said. "Get up. We've got to follow him."

"Follow him?" she said. She stopped rocking and stared up at me. "Are you out of your mind? There is no way I am going to follow a man who cuts up white ladies for fun. No. No way."

"Come on," I said, my voice urgent. "We're going to lose him if you don't hurry up."

"Did you not hear what I just said? I said I am not following no murdering crazy man. No."

"If you don't come with me, I'm going straight to your Maw-Maw's house and tell her that you have stopped helping me."

"You think my Maw-Maw wants me following crazy killer men?"

"I think she wants you to help me."

Ashara whooshed out an angry breath. "Dammit. Now you got me mad enough that I ain't even scared."

"Good. Come on."

She stood up, shaking her head and brushing off her pants, and followed me to the back door.

"Now wait here while I check it out," I said. I stuck my head out through the door and looked up and down the alleyway. The man was just now finishing his own inspection of the street and stepping out of the alley. I slipped back into the room.

"You have got to quit doing that," Ashara said. "It's downright unnerving."

I ignored her comment. "He just walked out to the street. We can go now."

Ashara unlocked and opened the door slowly so as to make no sound. I preceded her into the alley and motioned her out behind me. We moved quickly down the alley. When we got to the corner, I motioned her back against the wall while I looked around the corner in the direction the man had gone.

I was just in time to see him get into a white SUV and pull away from the curb. He hadn't parked far from where Ashara's car was.

I waited until he turned a corner, and then said, "Okay. Now. Move quickly."

We ran to Ashara's car and got in. As we pulled up to the corner, I said, "He turned right here."

"Tell me again why I'm doing this," Ashara said, turning the corner.

"Because your Maw-Maw would have your hide if you didn't," I said.

She shook her head and started the car. "Not that. The part where I'm driving a ghost lady around."

"There he is," I said. "Up ahead. In that white SUV."

"I mean," Ashara continued, "you're a ghost. Can't you just, I don't know, teleport yourself over there or something?"

"Get up closer to him," I said. "I want to get the license plate."

Luckily for us, he had chosen to take the main street through Abramsville. It's a small enough town that it pretty much shuts down at night, with the exception of the main drag--the street that hosts all of the fast-food chains, restaurants, pharmacies, and, of course, the twenty-four hour Wal-Mart. There were enough people still out that we were able to stay a couple of cars behind the SUV.

"Are you listening to me at all?" Ashara asked. "Why don't you just teleport your ass over there and let me go home?"

"Teleport?"

"Yeah. You know. Like they do on Star Wars."

"I think that was Star Trek."

"Whatever. You're here, then you're there. Then you ride with him and you see where he's going."

"I don't know, Ashara. I don't know what I can do."

"Seems to me like maybe you haven't been practicing all your ghosting stuff."

"I don't even know what 'ghosting stuff' is," I said, throwing my hands up into the air and shaking my head.

Ashara shook her head. "You get me killed and my

Maw-Maw's gonna have both our hides."

"Just get closer to him, okay?"

She pulled up directly behind the SUV and I repeated the license plate to myself several times until I was sure I'd remember it.

"Okay," I said. "You can fall back some more now."

"What was he doing in there?" Ashara asked.

"I don't know. He picked up something from the bench and put it in his pocket."

"Didn't you look to see what it was?"

"I didn't have time to get over there."

"'Cause you don't know if you can teleport 'cause you ain't bothered practicing being a ghost," Ashara said sarcastically.

That's when I realized where we were. The SUV was still two or three cars ahead of us, and he was just passing the city limits sign.

"Oh, hell," I said.

"What?" Ashara asked, sudden panic in her voice.

"Just keep following him, okay? Don't let him see you. Don't get caught. Just follow him as far as you. . . ."

And then--*pop!* I was standing in the middle of downtown Abramsville, Alabama. I paced back and forth, sometimes floating, sometimes walking, trying to figure out how to get back in touch with Ashara. The courthouse has a statue of some Civil War general in front of it--I think it's a requisite item in downtown squares in the Deep South. In the end, I got bored with pacing and floated up to rest on top of it.

So there I was, sitting on the shoulders of General Whosit, waiting for the only sane psychic in Abramsville, Alabama to figure out what had happened and come get me.

To be honest, I was worried about her--she was out there chasing some murdering freak and no one knew where she was--but I couldn't figure out what to do about it.

Then I remembered Maw-Maw. I might not know where Ashara was, but I would bet that Maw-Maw hadn't left her house since the last time I'd seen her.

Yeah. I know. I'm a little slow sometimes.

I made my way as quickly as possible back over to Maw-Maw's. And in the process, I discovered something new about all that "ghosting stuff." Ashara was right. I couldn't exactly teleport, but I could cover ground pretty damn quickly. It was a lot like flying. Guess I could have ridden along in the SUV after all--at least to the city limits.

I flew right on in to Maw-Maw's living room. She was there; fast asleep in her reclining chair, television still on.

"Mrs. Jones?" I whispered. Maw-Maw didn't move. "Mrs. Jones," I said more loudly. I waited a minute. No response. "Mrs. Jones!" This time I virtually shouted.

"I heard you the first time," she said, opening her eyes. "But I ain't no Mrs. Jones." I started to apologize, but she held her hand up to stop me.

"Jones was my daughter's husband," she said. "And let me tell you something. He wasn't no good at all. Couldn't keep a job to save his life. So don't you go calling me no 'Mrs. Jones.' My name is Adelaide Thompkins."

I nodded. "Okay, then, Mrs. Thompkins. I need to know if your granddaughter has a cell phone."

Maw-Maw looked thoughtful. "I don't know about that, but she got one of them phones she can carry with her."

"Thank God," I sighed. "Could you call her on it for me?"

Maw-Maw looked at me suspiciously. "You get my baby in trouble?"

By this time, I was hopping from foot to ethereal foot. "I sure hope not."

Maw-Maw nodded at me. "Yep. She's in some kind of trouble, ain't she?"

She put her hands on the arms of her chair and pushed herself up. I placed my hand against her back to help steady her before realizing that it wouldn't do any good, anyway.

"Now where is that telephone?" she muttered to

herself, peering through her thick glasses around the room.

"It's there," I said, pointing at an end-table beside the couch.

"Ah. So it is." She made her slow, arthritic way over to the phone and picked it up. "Now," she said. "You're going to have to tell me which number it is, honey." She held out the phone for me to look at. The electronic display was oversized, but apparently still too small for Maw-Maw to see clearly.

"Okay," I said, examining the phone. "Push the asterisk key down there at the bottom, then push number two."

"You mean the star?"

"Yes. The star." I tried to keep the panic out of my voice. I knew that the longer Ashara followed the killer, the more likely he was to catch on to her.

Maw-Maw put the phone up to her ear. I waited impatiently as it rang once, twice. And then I blew out a breath of relief when Ashara answered. I leaned in close to hear what she was saying.

"Maw-Maw," she said, her voice worried. "Why are you calling me this late? What's wrong?"

"It's your white ghost lady," Maw-Maw said. "She wants to talk to you." She tried to pass me the phone, but it moved through my outstretched hand without even a pause.

"Oh," said Maw-Maw. "I guess she can't, though."

"What's she doing there?" Ashara asked.

"I don't know," Maw-Maw said. She looked up at me.

"I was worried about you and didn't know where else to go," I said.

"If you're so worried, why'd you leave?" Ashara asked, her voice acerbic.

"I didn't mean to. I just can't go outside the city limits."

"Well. That would have been nice to know," Ashara said.

"Where are you now?"

"I'm at home, getting ready for bed."

"Did you find anything out?"

"Yep. I followed him all the way to a dirt road, and then I quit, 'cause it was just me and him and I wasn't about to let him cut me up."

"That's good," I said. "Why don't I come over and we can--"

Ashara cut me off. "Nope. I've got to work tomorrow and I am going to bed. We can talk about it later."

"But . . ." I said.

"You still there, Maw-Maw?" Ashara asked.

"Yeah, baby, I'm still here."

"You go on back to bed. I'll be over tomorrow to check on you."

"Okay, baby," Maw-Maw said. "Goodnight." And then she hung up the phone.

I heaved a huge sigh.

"You might as well just go on, now," Maw-Maw said. "Looks like there ain't no more time for ghosty things tonight."

I stared at her.

"Go on. Get."

Shaking my head, I walked out of the house. Through the wall.

Ghosty things, indeed.

Chapter Seven

Ashara jumped and nearly screamed the next morning when I popped in beside her at her teller's window. She suppressed the scream, though, managing to hold it down to a gasping squeak.

"You okay?" the teller next to her asked.

"I'm fine," she said. "I just almost dropped this." She waved the wad of paper in her hand. The other teller nodded and went back to her own work. Ashara's cash drawer was open and she was counting money, her fingers flying over the ten-key pad to her right, then clicking across the keyboard in front of her. She moved so quickly I could hardly follow what she was doing. Numbers scrolled across the screen of the computer monitor to her right.

"So where did he turn off the main road last night?" I asked Ashara. She studiously ignored me. Not that she could answer me directly, what with the other teller standing right next to her.

Time for Twenty Questions.

"Did he stay on the main highway?"

Ashara nodded, as if bobbing her head to some internal music.

"Doesn't I-20 cross that highway?" I asked. She kept bobbing her head, fingers dancing across the two keyboards, numbers running down the monitor.

"Did he go past the interstate, then?" I asked. Her head-bob turned into a shake. No, then.

"Did he turn left or right?"

Ashara's head stilled completely. Oops. Yes or no questions only, I reminded myself.

"Left?" No movement.

"Right?" A bob of the head.

"Could you get back there?" Another head bob.

Not that I was sure I wanted her going back out there alone. Really, what I wanted to do was go check the place out myself. But I was stuck in town.

"So what time do you get off work?" I asked Ashara.

Her hand stilled, and then her fingers popped up off the keyboard.

"Four?" I asked.

She nodded.

Four o'clock. That was hours and hours away. I practically hummed with frustration. "Can't you get off work any earlier?"

Ashara went back to shaking her head.

So I left Ashara and went to explore the rest of the bank.

Small-town bank branches are boring. There's not much to them, really. But I did practice exerting my combo hand-mind tug on physical objects.

This time when I moved up to Ashara from behind, she didn't react at all.

"Yes, ma'am," she was saying into the microphone. "You have a nice day." The woman in the car outside the window smiled at her and pulled away.

"You know," I said conversationally, "I just figured out how to open safe deposit boxes."

Ashara turned to me, her eyes wide. I could see her trying to figure out some way to talk to me without her coworkers overhearing.

"Oh, don't worry," I said cheerfully, "I closed them all up again. But I think I'm getting better at moving things." I popped open her cash drawer, just to demonstrate. She slammed it shut again.

"Quit that," she hissed out of the corner of her mouth.

"What was that, Ashara?" the other teller asked.

"Nothing," Ashara said calmly. "Just a cough."

"We could make a fortune," I said. "Ashara Jones and Callie Taylor, bank robbers. Of course, it would be a short career, since I can't leave Abramsville. And they'd probably catch us. Or you, anyway."

Ashara sighed, tilted her head, and looked at me.

"Hey, Ann," she said to the other teller. "I'm going to go grab a quick bathroom break while it's quiet. Cover for me?"

"No problem," said Ann.

She turned and surreptitiously waved her hand for me to follow her. We walked into the ladies' restroom and she finally turned to face me head-on.

"Go away," she said. "I'm trying to work here."

"But we need to figure out what to do next."

"Look, Callie," she said, and then she stopped. "You know what? I think I liked it better before I knew your name. I liked you better as White Ghost Lady."

"Yeah, well, I do have a name. Callie Elaine Taylor. I may be a ghost, but I'm a real person, too."

Ashara sighed. "Okay, Callie Elaine Taylor," she said. "Why don't you go do something useful while I'm working? You're getting so good at moving things, you ought to go back to the music shop and see if you can find anything."

Ooh. The shop. I'd gotten so excited about finding the man that I'd forgotten about the shop. "Okay," I said, nodding eagerly.

"Come back at four," Ashara said. "I'll talk to you then."

*   *   *   *

The music repair shop was much as I remembered it, except that this time it was full of people. It hadn't occurred to me that Rick's shop would continue operating with Rick in jail awaiting trial, but apparently his employees were keeping things running in his absence.

I moved in through the front door this time, since I didn't have Ashara with me. A young, blond, bearded man stood at the front counter, bent over the case polishing some piece of metal--it looked like it might belong to a trumpet or something.

I drifted past him--he never looked up--and into the

back room. The workbenches were occupied by three people working on instruments. One young, thin man was carefully sanding a piece of wood. He had a violin propped up in front of him. A second man, this one burly and broad and red in the face, worked a small soldering iron against two pieces of metal. I had no idea what that was for. And finally, an older woman with grey-streaked blonde hair carefully tapped against the dents in a trombone.

But one bench stood empty. The one the man had taken something from the night before. I stood in front of it, staring down at the array of things in front of me. Some of them were clearly tools. Others were clearly parts of musical instruments. And yet others held no meaning for me, jumbles of metal and wood and glue. I ran my eyes across it again and again, inventorying the items. None of them seemed to have any bearing on Molly's murder.

And then I glanced down at the small trash can beside the bench. There, inside it, lay a small piece of piano wire. It looked just like the wire the man had used to kill Molly.

I'd watched a lot of television in the past few months. I'd seen just about every episode of *CSI*. Twice. And I knew that if this was from the same spool of wire used to kill Molly McClatchey, a lab could match the cut ends. And I knew that if it had anyone else's DNA on it, it might cast doubt on Rick's guilt.

What I didn't know was how to get it out of the workshop. I mean, I could pop open drawers, turn bolt locks, and make bells ring, but all of those things were short-term events. And they took a lot out of me. I didn't think I could get the wire out of the trash can and all the way to Ashara. Certainly not with all these people around.

Just then, the bearded man from the front of the shop walked to the doorway of the workroom.

"Excuse me," he said, "but I can help you?" He had a deep voice, deeper than I would have expected.

I continued staring into the trash can, trying to figure

out how to get it to the police. Everyone else looked up at him.

"Nope," the woman said. "I've almost got this damn thing straightened out." The rest of the repairmen went back to work.

The young man shook his head. "I'm sorry, ma'am," he said, moving into the room, "but you can't be back here."

"Ha, ha," said the woman, not looking up from her trombone. "Very funny, Stephen."

Stephen looked at her, then shook his head again, his eyebrows knitted in confusion. He took several more steps into the room.

That's when I realized that he was talking to me.

I looked at his face, my eyes huge.

"Can I help you?" he asked again. His colleagues looked up again.

"What the hell is wrong with you?" the burly man asked irritably.

"Oh," I said. "Yes. Actually, you can help me. Let's go to the front." I scurried out of the workroom before poor Stephen had time to say anything else. No need to make his colleagues think he was totally crazy.

Once we were in the showroom again, I glanced around to make sure no one else was within earshot.

"Whose workbench was that?" I asked.

He stared at me suspiciously. "Why do you want to know?"

Good question.

"Well," I said hesitatingly, "I'm a friend of Rick's. And Molly's. And I don't think Rick did it."

"I don't either," Stephen said.

"So I was just wondering if there was anyone who might have something against either of them."

"You know, the police have already been here and asked all those questions," Stephen said.

"What did you tell them?"

"Who did you say you were again?" Stephen asked.

"A friend."

He just stared at me.

I sighed.

"My name is Callie Taylor. I'm a friend of Rick's. I really am just trying to help."

"So why do you want to know whose workbench that is?"

I thought about it for a second, then took a deep breath and said it. "Because there's a length of piano wire in the trash can. If it's from the same spool that killed Molly, the police might be able to do something with it. Maybe they could prove it wasn't Rick."

Stephen's eyes narrowed. "Really?"

I shrugged. "It's worth a try."

Stephen headed back to the workroom.

"Don't touch it!" I called out after him. "Just bring the whole can!"

He nodded in acknowledgment.

He came back in, staring down into the trash can. "So what should we do?" he asked.

"Maybe call the police?" I suggested.

"Yeah. Good idea," he said. He picked up the phone.

"So whose bench is it?" I asked again, just before his fingers touched the number pad.

"Jeffrey McClatchey," he said. "Rick's brother."

*   *   *   *

I left the shop while Stephen was on the phone with the police. No need to get him thrown into a mental ward for talking to The Woman Who Wasn't There.

But I did stick close by. In fact, I slipped into the back seat of one of the two police cruisers that had shown up. I wanted to see what they did next.

In the meantime, I thought about what kind of sicko Rick's brother would have to be to strangle Molly and then cut her up like that. At least the sick fuck who'd killed me had been the "Stranger" in Stranger Danger. I hadn't ever seen him before that awful night when he'd grabbed me.

After about half an hour, the cops came back out of Rick's shop.

"We'll take this to the lab in Birmingham," one of them said, waving an evidence bag. "Why don't you two go back to Jeffrey McClatchey and see if he's changed his story any." Two of the other policemen nodded and headed toward their patrol car.

The other patrol car.

Dammit. I wanted to see Jeffrey McClatchey. Besides, I couldn't go to Birmingham even if I wanted to.

I slid across the seat, out of the car, and dove through the back passenger door of the other police cruiser just as it pulled out from in front of the store. I sat up in the back seat and looked out the window to see Stephen staring at me, his eyes enormous and his face as white as a--well, not ghost, 'cause I'm not especially pale. Let's go with sheet. A white one. Not a floral printed one.

I guessed that he had seen my little non-corporeal cruiser-switching act.

I would have bet almost anything that he was heading back to the workroom to ask his co-workers about the woman who had been looking at Jeffrey's workbench.

Poor guy.

I sat in the back of the patrol car, unsure whether or not to hope that Jeffrey McClatchey was the killer. How awful that would be for Rick.

I also spent some time hoping that if it was McClatchey, the police cruiser wouldn't go outside the city limits and leave me popped back into the middle of the downtown square.

But I really didn't have enough time to hope much of anything at all for very long, because after a few moments, the patrol car pulled into a brand-new subdivision on the edge of town. The houses all had brick facades and siding on the sides. Nice, but not extravagant. If this was where Jeffrey

McClatchey lived, he was doing well, but not as well as his brother. Rick and Molly lived in a huge remodeled Colonial-style home. Then again, this was small-town Alabama, not Dallas. Houses in Dallas were much more expensive.

I followed the two cops up to the front door, glad that they weren't able to see me. The taller of the two rang the doorbell, and after a long pause, a man in his mid- to late-thirties answered the door. He wore sweatpants and a t-shirt, and his hair stood up in the back, as if he had been asleep. His eyes were rimmed in red.

My shoulders slumped, but I wasn't sure if it was in relief or disappointment. This was not the man who had killed Molly McClatchey.

"Yeah?" he asked, scratching his chest through his t-shirt.

"Mr. McClatchey?" The taller officer spoke first

"Yes." Jeffrey McClatchey stared at the cops through slitted eyes.

"May we come in for a moment and talk to you?"

"I've already told you everything I know," he said. He sounded almost belligerent.

"There have been some new developments and we'd like to discuss them with you," the shorter officer said.

McClatchey sighed and opened the door wider. "Okay. Fine. Come on in."

Chapter Eight

I didn't bother to follow the three men into McClatchey's house. I already knew he wasn't the killer.

I checked the clock in the patrol car on my way by. Noon. Way too early to go get Ashara.

But maybe she'll be on her lunch break, I thought.

No such luck. This time when I popped through the bullet-proof (but not ghost-proof!) window, she just started singing quietly to herself. Or rather, to me, but no one else would know that.

"Go on now, go, walk out the door. Just turn around now, you're not welcome anymore," she sang.

"You've been working on that all morning, haven't you?" I said.

She grinned a little, nodding.

Then I picked up the song. "Weren't you the one who tried to hurt me with goodbye? Did you think I'd crumble, did you think I'd lay down and die?" I danced across the room. "Oh, no, not I!"

Ashara cringed and shuddered.

Okay. So maybe I'm not the best singer in the world. And maybe I don't have the greatest rhythm. But she didn't have to shudder.

"I went back to the shop," I said, as Ashara leaned into her microphone and pushed a button.

"Good afternoon," she said to the man driving the car.

"Hello," he replied, sending the plastic container through the tube. It popped up into a box-shaped space next to Ashara's elbow. She pushed a button and the cover flipped open. I watched with interest as she pulled the container out of the box and opened it.

"I always thought that was so cool when I was a kid," I said.

"Just turn around now, you're not welcome anymore," she sang under her breath as she began counting money. Her fingers flew over the keypads.

"I found some more piano wire," I said. "In the trash can next to the bench the killer took something from. I got one of the guys working there to call the police."

Her fingers slowed and she looked at me, eyebrows raised.

"He could see me," I said, waving my hand dismissively. "But no one else could. He didn't know that, though. He thought I was real. Alive, I mean. I am real. I think he saw me walk through the police car door, though. So now maybe he thinks he's crazy."

Ashara shook her head and went back to work. She dropped the container into the box, closed the lid, and pushed a button. "Is there anything else I can do for you today?" she asked, leaning into her microphone.

"No, ma'am," the man in the car said.

"Have a nice day, Mr. Johnston," she said.

"So I was thinking," I said. Ashara didn't even look at me. She just moved on to the next car in her line.

"Hello," she said.

"Hi," the driver replied.

"I was thinking that what we need to do now is figure out how to track down that man's license plate number."

Ashara stopped and looked at me out of the corner of her eye. Her mouth tightened and she held up four fingers, flexing them emphatically in my direction.

"You okay?" Ann, the other teller, asked.

"Just stretching my fingers," Ashara said. She pulled the container from the box and took several checks from the container. She typed in a code and began entering the checks into the computer.

"Okay, okay," I said. "I get it. I'll come back at four."

I walked out through the door, singing "I Will Survive" at the top of my lungs. I glanced back to see Ashara shuddering again.

*   *   *   *

When Ashara got off work at 4:00, I was already waiting in her car. I had managed to turn the radio on and was listening to NPR radio. Ashara got in and switched the radio off.

"Hey," I said. "It took me a long time to turn that on."

"And it only took me a second to turn it off again," she said. "We have to talk."

"Okay," I said. "What?"

"Look. I am helping you because . . . I don't know why. Because Maw-Maw said to, I guess. But mostly 'cause you won't leave me alone. But I do not need you showing up at my work. I am busy when I'm there and I ain't got no time to talk to your dead ass."

I looked at her for a minute, my eyes narrowing. "Why is it," I asked, "that you speak in complete, grammatically correct sentences sometimes and other times you say things like 'ain't got no time'?"

Ashara drew in a long breath and blew it out in an even longer sigh. "That is not what we're discussing right now."

"Okay, okay," I said. "I won't bother you at work again."

"Good."

"Unless it's really, really necessary."

"How necessary?"

"I don't know. Like someone else has died or something."

She nodded.

"But you have to answer my question."

"What question?" she asked.

"Why is it that sometimes you speak correctly and sometimes you don't?"

She shook her head. "It's called code switching," she said, her voice suddenly sounding almost professorial. "And it's not a matter of correct or incorrect. It's a matter of dialect. People who function in more than one world can switch back and forth at will. At work, I have to use the dominant discourse--I have to sound like a white woman. At home, I speak the way I was brought up to speak."

I stared at her with my mouth hanging open.

"I learned it in my socio-linguistics course in college." She shrugged. "It made perfect sense to me, so it stuck."

She started the car and pulled out onto the street.

"What was your major?" I asked, trying not to sound as shocked as I felt. And embarrassed. I had made a set of assumptions about Ashara that clearly wasn't correct.

"Accounting," she said. "I was good at it, too. I had a 4.0 GPA in my major. 3.5 overall."

I tried to phrase my next question very carefully. "So why don't you work as an accountant somewhere?"

"No jobs like that around here. Except at tax time. I do people's taxes to make a little extra money sometimes."

"But with those sorts of grades, surely you could have gotten a job in Birmingham or Atlanta," I said. "Why are you here working as a bank teller?"

She shook her head. "Maw-Maw's the only family I've got left, and she's lived in Abramsville all her life. I can't make her go with me, so I stay right here."

I nodded. I understood that. I'd turned down a promotion once because it would have meant moving to Chicago, and I didn't want to be that far from my family. Then I shook my head to dispel the memory, unwilling to think about my family. That would only lead to wondering how they were dealing with my death.

"So what next?" Ashara asked.

"Next we go find out who that license plate is registered to."

"Don't we need to go to the DMV for that? I don't think they're gonna let some random chick and her ghost friend just go on in and look it up."

"I think we can get that stuff over the internet," I said.
"No way!"
"I'm pretty sure. You got internet at your place?"

Ashara nodded. "Of course."

"Let's go then."

*   *   *   *

Ashara's house was small, but in a better neighborhood than her grandmother's. "I got it pretty cheap," she said as she unlocked the front door. "The guy who owned it had rented it out to a bunch of college kids and the inside was trashed. Way nasty. But I cleaned it out and been fixing it up a little bit at a time. I still got stuff to do, but it's not bad."

'Not bad' was an understatement. The outside of the house was a modest little A-frame, but the interior was beautiful. The walls were painted a creamy matte beige and the window and door frames were a bright white. Folk art adorned the walls, adding bright splashes of color to the room. The wood floors were polished to a bright shine and colorful rugs scattered across the room complemented the art.

"This is lovely," I said, staring around at the living room.

"Have a seat," Ashara said. "I'd offer you something to drink, but . . ." her voice trailed off.

"Yeah," I said. "But. On accounta I'm dead and all."

"Yeah, that. I'm going to go change clothes. I'll be back in a minute."

When she returned she had traded her black slacks and blue button-down shirt for a pair of gray sweatpants and a black t-shirt.

"The computer's back here," she said, leading me to a guest room. She sat down and I drifted up behind her.

"So where should we start?" she asked. She clicked the mouse and pulled up a web browser.

"I don't know," I said. "I guess maybe run a search for license plate registration?"

Ashara typed in the search terms, hit "search," and waited while the page loaded. Then she let out a low whistle. "Damn, girl. Is it really that easy?" she asked. The result page showed link after link to sites promising to allow you to instantly find license plate registration information.

She clicked on the first one. "Nope," she said. "I ain't paying no $99.95 just to find this out."

"He killed a woman, Ashara," I said. "If I could pay it, I would. But I can't."

Ashara looked up at me.

"He chopped her up, Ashara. He left her body in the bathtub with all the pieces carefully arranged."

"God, stop!" Ashara put her hand up, palm facing me. "I didn't say I wouldn't pay for it at all. I said I wasn't going to pay a hundred bucks. Geez. Let's do a little comparison shopping before we start spending all my hard-earned cash, okay?"

"Okay." I sighed in relief.

Ashara ran through several sites before finding one that satisfied her. "See? Twenty dollars, now that I can afford. Let me go find my purse."

I hovered anxiously over the computer, waiting for Ashara to get back. We were close to finding out who had killed Molly. I didn't know how we were going to get the information to the police, but I was sure we could.

Ashara returned, credit card in hand. "Okay," she said, after setting up her account with the online company. "What was the number?"

I repeated it to her, she typed it in, and we both stared intently at the screen.

I let out a whoosh of non-breath when the results came up. "Dammit," I said.

"Yeah," said Ashara. "I don't think that was no seventy-two year old woman named Juana Nogales driving a Chevrolet Cavalier the other night."

"Maybe he's related to her somehow?" I surmised. "Grandmother, maybe?"

"More likely he stole the plates and switched them out," Ashara said.

I put my head in my hands. "I was so sure we had

him."

Ashara reached over to pat me on the back, and then stopped herself before she put her hand through me. "Look," she said. "I need to go check in on Maw-Maw. Why don't you come with me? Maybe we can think of something on the way over there."

*   *   *   *

Maw-Maw was still in her recliner. "Well," she said as we came in through the front door. "I see you still got you that white lady ghost."

"Yep," said Ashara. "We can't seem to find out enough about that guy to go to the police with it."

Maw-Maw snorted. "What you think you gonna tell the police anyway? That you know that man killed that woman 'cause a spirit told you so?"

"We hadn't gotten that far," I said, sitting down on the couch. "First we've got to find out who he is, then we can figure out what to tell the police."

"Tell me what you know," Maw-Maw said.

So I did. Everything. Well, almost everything. I didn't go into graphic detail about the man cutting up the body or anything. No need to frighten the old lady.

Ashara had moved into the kitchen, where I heard her opening cabinets and cans, pulling out dishes.

"Ashara, honey?" Maw-Maw called.

"Yeah?"

"Where'd that killer man turn off the main road?"

"Onto some dirt road," she called from the kitchen. "Before the interstate, but after you pass your doctor's office."

"Hmm." Maw-Maw nodded to herself. "That sure sounds like the road out to the old Howard place."

Ashara came into the room with two plates of food-- roast chicken, creamed spinach, and cornbread, and it all smelled wonderful--and set one of them down on the end table next to Maw-Maw's chair. She took the other one over to the end table next to the couch and moved back into the kitchen.

She came out a moment later with two glasses of iced tea and sat down on the couch.

"What you want to watch on the TV, Maw-Maw?" she asked.

"I don't want to watch nothing right now. I want to talk more about this murder case you girls are working on."

"Maw-Maw, this is not like one of your crime shows," Ashara said. "We are not working on any 'case.' I'm just trying to help Callie here out."

"Oh. So the white ghost lady got a name now, does she?"

"Yes, ma'am," I said. "I'm Callie Taylor. I'm here from Dallas." It's amazing how quickly southern training kicks back in. I can be a total bitch, but you put me in a room with an old woman, and suddenly it's all "yes, ma'am, no, ma'am."

And I don't care what Ashara says. Dallas is still the South.

"And you, young lady," Maw-Maw said, suddenly turning on Ashara, "don't you go acting like I don't know the difference between my TV stories and real life. I been alive plenty long enough to know what's what. And just 'cause I'm old and half-blind don't mean I'm senile. Not yet."

"Yes, ma'am," Ashara said meekly.

"Now. What did that man look like?" Maw-Maw asked, turning back to me.

I described the man to her.

"Yep," she said. "That sure does sound like one of them Howard boys. Bad skin, every one of them." She shook her head. "They never was no good. Always in one kind of trouble or another. Not nothing like this before, mind you. Not murder. Not that nobody ever found out about, anyway."

I leaned forward avidly. "You think that maybe there was something that nobody knew about?"

Maw-Maw nodded. "There was rumors. When I was just a girl, Jimmy Powell just up and disappeared. Prettiest boy you ever saw. My momma thought maybe he was gonna marry me someday, but Jimmy Powell was just a big ol' flirt. Didn't mean nothing by it." She smiled as she reminisced.

"Anyway," she said, "Jimmy Powell went missing one day. His people said he hadn't just run away. They said he'd gotten into a fight with one of them Howard boys. They was pretty sure them Howard boys had done dragged Jimmy Powell off and done him in. Now what was their names?" She stroked her chin as she tried to remember. "Oh, yes," she said. "Graham and Owen Howard. That's who they was. Owen was always the meanest one." She shook her head sadly. "Anyway, not much came of it. Colored boy gone missing? Sheriff didn't pay much attention to Jimmy's people. Said Jimmy must've gotten himself in trouble with some girl and run off. Either that or gone to look for work someplace else. But Jimmy's people knew better. We all did. Jimmy wouldn't have left without telling his momma goodbye."

Ashara and I both leaned forward, listening intently. Ashara had completely forgotten the food on her plate.

"Like I said," said Maw-Maw, shaking off her reverie, "them Howard boys are no good. You watch out for this man. If he's a Howard, there ain't no telling what he might do." She reached over and picked up her plate of food.

"Maybe you girls can just take me out there after we're done eating. That way I can tell you for sure if it's the old Howard place. Yep." She nodded to herself. "That's what we're gonna do."

Ashara and I stared at each other in mutual horror.

Chapter Nine

"Maw-Maw," Ashara said, "I don't think that's such a good idea."

"I have to agree with Ashara, Mrs. Thompkins," I said.

Maw-Maw reached out and patted at my hand on my lap, ignoring the fact that her hand went right through mine.

"You can call me Miss Adelaide," she said. "All Ashara's friends do."

"Okay, then, Miss Adelaide," I said. "I don't think it's a good idea for you to go out there. That man is dangerous. He's already killed once. I saw it, Miss Adelaide, and it was horrible. He is cold blooded. He won't hesitate a minute to kill you, too."

"Well, then," said Maw-Maw, "we'll just have to take us some protection. Ashara, you go into my second-best bedroom and look in the bureau in there. Third drawer down. There's a gun and some bullets. You just bring those in here and we'll take them with us."

Ashara's eyes grew enormous. "A gun? Maw-Maw, I didn't know you had a gun."

Maw-Maw rested her hands on her stomach complacently. "No need for you to know before now. Go on back there and get it."

Ashara looked at me with huge eyes. I shrugged. Maw-Maw was her grandmother. Hell if I knew what to do about her.

Ashara left the room and came back moments later with a pearl-handled handgun. It looked like a snub-nosed .38 double-action revolver, but I couldn't be sure unless I got a closer look at it.

I grew up in Texas. I know guns. I'd handled them much of my life. So what? It didn't do me a damn bit of good when my own killer grabbed me. But believe me, if I'd been carrying, I'd have shot that bastard dead on the spot without so much as a flinch.

Ashara clearly didn't know guns; she handled it like it was a live snake that might bite her at any minute.

"Well, give it to me," Maw-Maw said. Ashara handed it over gingerly.

Maw-Maw, on the other hand, handled the gun like a pro. Her hands shook with age, but she popped open the cylinder and checked the rounds already loaded inside. She nodded, apparently satisfied with what she saw, and clicked the cylinder back into place.

"How long have you had that thing?" Ashara asked, shaking her head in amazement.

"Oh, your Grampa gave it to me years ago. Just in case I ever needed it. Now it looks like I just might."

"I don't mean to intrude here," I said, "but when was the last time that gun was cleaned?" I could just see it backfiring in Maw-Maw's face.

"I got my yard boy to clean it for me just last month," Maw-Maw said. "He did a right fine job of it, too. Sat here and watched him do it."

"You paid a fifteen-year-old boy to clean your gun?" Ashara's voice went up several notches by the end of her sentence.

"Sure did," said Maw-Maw. "Now. Where's my cane? I want to get back in time for *Law and Order* at eight o'clock." She started hauling herself up out of her chair. Ashara grabbed her elbow and handed her a wooden cane from beside the chair.

"There's a little problem," I said. They both stopped and stared at me. "I can't seem to leave the city limits. Every time I try to, I just end up back in the downtown square."

Maw-Maw's eyes narrowed. "Hmm," she said. "Seems like there ought to be a way to keep that from happening. You just come on with us and we'll see what we can do."

At this point, I wasn't about to miss out on any part of this little adventure unless I absolutely had to, so I followed them out to Ashara's car, watching as Ashara helped Maw-

Maw into the passenger seat.

We moved out onto the main road and headed north toward the interstate. I looked at Rick's repair shop as we passed through the square and wondered briefly about the poor guy who had seen me dive through the closed car doors. Then we were on the main drag and heading past all the fast food restaurants.

"Okay," I finally said. "When we hit the city limits, I'll end up back in the square. So I'll meet y'all back at Miss Adelaide's house when you're done."

"Don't you go making up your mind so fast, missy," Maw-Maw said. "Ashara, give me your hand."

Ashara glanced over at her, frowning.

"Just one hand," Maw-Maw said. "You can keep the other on the steering wheel."

"Well, that's a relief," muttered Ashara.

"And you can just watch that smart mouth, too. Don't think you're so big that I can't still smack you."

Ashara grinned and reached her right hand out to her grandmother. Maw-Maw took it and held it up toward me.

"Now," she said to me. "You just put your hand on ours."

I looked at her suspiciously. "You know my hand is going to go right through yours."

Maw-Maw just stared at me.

I sighed. "Fine." I reached out and let my hand hover just above theirs.

"No," Maw-Maw said. "You gotta touch us. You just reach on in and hang on."

"Okay," I said, my voice distrustful. But I let my hand sink into their clasped grip. I felt a shiver run up my arm.

"Good," said Maw-Maw. "Everybody just hang on tight until we get past them city limits." She closed her eyes and leaned back into the seat.

I watched as we approached the city limits sign. As we pulled past it, I felt suddenly disoriented, dizzy. I closed my eyes and felt a long sort of stretch at the center of what used to be my stomach, as if I were being pulled in two different directions.

Then I felt the *pop!* I had been waiting for all along. I opened my eyes, expecting to find myself in the Abramsville town square. Instead, I was right where I had been--in the back seat of Ashara's car. I pulled my hand away from Maw-Maw's and Ashara's clasped grip and leaned back against the seat.

"What the hell did you just do?" I asked.

"And you can just watch your mouth, too, young lady," Maw-Maw said to me. "Just 'cause you're dead don't mean I ain't got ways to get to you."

"Clearly," I muttered.

Ashara shook her head. "Okay. That was weird. What did you do, Maw-Maw?"

Maw-Maw turned her head and looked out the window. "Just thought about how much we wanted Callie here to come with us." She stated it as if it were the obvious answer.

"Oh. Well, then," I said. "Okay." Ashara met my glance in the rearview mirror and we shook our heads at each other.

We drove along for a few more minutes in silence. Then Ashara said, "It's the next road on the right, I think."

Maw-Maw nodded. "Yep. That would be the road to the old Howard place."

We turned onto it, Ashara's car rumbling and bumping over the dirt road. It hadn't rained in a while, but the road was not well cared for, so it was dried into a series of miniature gullies and hills.

"This better be worth it," Ashara said as she tried to avoid the worst of the ruts.

The road might have been the "old Howard place" road, but there were more than a few houses scattered along it. Cars stood on blocks in front of houses that needed painting. As we passed by the old, run-down houses and trailers tucked back into the trees, I thought that this looked like the Deep South that was so often portrayed on television and in movies--economically depressed, backwards, more than a little frightening. No one sat in a rocking chair on a front porch polishing a shotgun and no one played "Dueling Banjos," but I don't think I would have been surprised if they had. We were only a few miles outside of clean, neat, tidy little Abramsville, but in some ways, this was a world apart.

Ashara slowed the car to a crawl as we peered out the windows, looking for the white SUV the man had been driving the night before.

The road came to a dead end at a huge, rambling old farmhouse. The house was in utter disrepair. The white paint had long ago almost all peeled away, leaving the weather-darkened wood exposed. The long, wrap-around porch sagged in places. Plywood boards covered several windows where the glass had broken out.

The white SUV stood in front of it.

"This is it," I said. "I'm going to go inside and see what I can find out."

"What should we do?" Ashara whispered.

"I don't know. You really don't have to wait for me, you know. I can meet you back at Miss Adelaide's," I said.

"No, ma'am," Maw-Maw said. "I want to know what you find as soon as you find it. You are not just sending me home now that I got you all the way out here."

I couldn't very well argue with her. "Then just drive down the road a little and wait for me."

"Why can't we just wait right here?" Maw-Maw demanded.

"Because, Maw-Maw," Ashara said in a fierce whisper, "his car is right here. He won't see Callie, but he's sure to notice us. Now let's get out of here."

"Uh-oh," I said as the front door of the house swung open. "It looks like he's already noticed us."

Molly McClatchey's killer stepped out onto the

sagging front porch and stared at us.

"Okay," I said. "I'm going inside. You fake him out. Tell him you're lost or something. Then get the hell out of here. I'll meet you at the end of the road."

I ducked out of the car before either Ashara or Maw-Maw could answer. The man walked toward the car.

"Can I help you?" he said. He didn't sound overly suspicious, I thought as Ashara rolled down her window.

"I'm looking for Jimmy Jones's place," she said in her strongest southern accent. "Do you know where he lives?"

"No, ma'am," he said. "I think you must have the wrong road." I moved toward the front door.

"Are you one of them Howard boys?" I heard Maw-Maw ask. I groaned. *No. No, no, no.* They needed to get out of here. I turned around to the car and waved them off with both hands. Ashara stared back and forth between me and her grandmother, but she didn't move the car.

Dammit.

I slipped into the house, deciding that it would be better for me to get in and back out to them quickly. Maybe that way Maw-Maw would shut up and we could all get out of here.

I could still hear them talking outside.

"Why do you want to know?" the man asked. Now his voice was suspicious.

"This is the old Howard place, ain't it? And you look just like your grand-daddy," Maw-Maw said.

The inside of the house was dim. Dust motes floated in the air, shining in the scant light that came in from the few un-boarded windows. It was neat, though. An old couch sat in one corner of the living room across from a television. A rolltop desk stood in the corner. A seventies-era coffee table completed the furnishings.

I moved to the rolltop desk. The top was down. I stuck my head through the cover, but it was too dark to see anything. Even at the time, I thought that seemed weird. A ghost ought to be able to see in the dark, don't you think? Well, I can't. Not the total pitch blackness of that desk, anyway.

I heard Ashara's car pulling away and sighed in relief.

The man came back into the house.

"Stupid nigger bitch," he muttered to himself as he moved through the living room. I bristled, wishing I could pick something up and hurl it at him. I even considered trying it for a moment--I was getting better at moving objects, after all--but in the end decided not to. The best way to get back at him would be to get him arrested for murder.

Now I just needed to know how.

I followed him into the kitchen, where he stood looking out the window at Ashara's retreating car.

Then he reached into his pocket and pulled something out. I moved in closer to him. He held a tiny key in his hand, staring down at it and bouncing it lightly in his hand. I leaned over and peered at it closely. He started a bit and shivered, looking around.

Crap. He was more sensitive than I had thought. He'd felt me.

He put the key back into his pocket and walked over to the telephone. I moved closer as he dialed, but caught only the last four numbers. 5478.

"Hey," he said into the receiver. "I think we need to move on this."

He was silent for a moment. "Sure. Tomorrow. Noon. See you there." He hung up the phone and began pacing through the house. Every so often he pulled the key back out of his pocket and fingered it.

Then he moved to the rolltop desk.

I knew it, I thought. There had to be something important in there.

He slid the top up and reached into one of the several cubby-holes in the desk. He pulled out a piece of paper. I leaned in over his shoulder and looked at it. It had just one number on it: 203. I moved back away. He shivered again, turning around to stare at where I'd been standing. Then he reached into desk again and grabbed another sheet of paper.

I was drifting forward again, trying to get a look at this sheet, when I felt a pulling sensation in my stomach, a stretching like I'd felt when we had passed the city limits. Then the *pop!*

And I was back in the back seat of Ashara's car.

"What the hell?" I said.

Ashara jumped and the car swerved.

"Don't do that," she said as she moved back into her lane.

"I didn't *do* anything," I said. "One minute I was watching the killer guy, the next minute I was back in the car."

"Hmm," said Maw-Maw thoughtfully.

"What?" I demanded.

"We just passed back into Abramsville when you showed up. Looks like maybe you can only leave the city limits when you're with us."

"Oh, God," I groaned.

"Don't you take the Lord's name in vain, young lady," Maw-Maw said.

"Does this mean I'm tied to you?" I asked, ignoring her admonishment.

"Maybe so," she replied, leaning back into the seat. "Or maybe to Ashara. Maybe both of us." She sounded all too complacent for my taste.

"Okay," I said, "not to be rude or anything, but if you and I are tied together, what happens when you die?"

"Well, I ain't planning on dying anytime soon," Maw-Maw said. Then she looked over her shoulder and smiled slyly. "But just maybe I'll drag your bony white ass up to heaven with me."

"Maw-Maw!" Ashara sounded shocked.

I spun in my seat and looked at my butt. "My ass is not bony!"

Maw-Maw just cackled and leaned back in her seat

again.

Chapter Ten

"So are we going to try to follow him tomorrow?" I asked as we pulled into Maw-Maw's driveway. Her house looked positively grand in comparison to the ones out on the old Howard place road.

"I have to work," Ashara said firmly. "I can't just quit going to work, even to catch a killer." Her voice shook slightly. "Anyway, he scares me. He has dead eyes. I think we ought to just go to the police and tell them what we know." She stepped out of the car and moved around to the passenger side to help Maw-Maw heave herself out of the car.

"They won't believe you," I said. "If you go in saying anything about this guy, they're going to want to know how you know he did it. And we don't have any proof at all."

Maw-Maw nodded as she hobbled up her front steps. "Callie's right, Ashara. You can't go talking to the police yet. And you can't let that Howard boy know what you know, so you gotta keep quiet for now."

Ashara sighed. "I still can't skip work. So you're just going to have to try to follow him yourself, Callie."

"How?" I almost wailed in frustration. "I can't even leave the city limits without one of you with me."

"I don't got to work," Maw-Maw said.

"No," said Ashara. "Absolutely not. Anyway, you can't drive anymore. You don't have a license."

Maw-Maw waved her hand in the air as if shooing that fact away. "Those people at the DMV don't have a lick of sense. I can see just fine to drive."

"You can not," Ashara said, opening the door. We all moved into the living room and Maw-Maw dropped into her seat with a huff.

"Furthermore," Ashara said, "you don't have a car, and I'm not letting you borrow mine." She crossed her arms and stood staring down at Maw-Maw implacably. Maw-Maw glared back at her granddaughter through her thick glasses.

Their expressions were remarkably similar.

The silence stretched out.

"I have an idea," I finally said.

*   *   *   *

I left Ashara at her house with the last four digits of the number that Howard had dialed. "I guess we just have to assume it's local," I said. "You ought to be able to find a reverse directory on the internet."

Ashara nodded as she wrote down the number, and then looked up at me doubtfully. "You sure you want to do this?" she asked.

I shrugged. "It's the only thing I can think of. You got any better ideas?"

She shook her head.

"Okay, then," I said. "I'll go see what I can find out. You do the same here. I'll be back in an hour or two."

I started at Rick McClatchey's musical instrument repair shop, back in the workroom. The store was closed and the lights were off, but I could see by the glint of moonlight coming in from the front window. Again I wondered briefly about the fact that I seemed to need some light to see.

Like I said, the living don't know jack about the dead.

Hell, I don't know jack about the dead, and I'm one of them.

I hovered over each of the workbenches, peering intently at the contents of each person's station as I tried to find something that would give me the information I needed.

Nothing.

I tried to pull open a file cabinet in the back, hoping to be able to riffle through some files. No luck. Apparently I could pop open money drawers at banks but not open plain old file cabinets.

I finally found what I was looking for under the counter at the back of the showroom. In a basket on a shelf, I discovered a pile of dusty name tags. And right on the top was the one I was looking for. Stephen Davenport.

Smiling triumphantly, I headed toward the front of the store. I was almost at the entrance when I heard a key slide into the back door.

I hate to admit it, but I froze in fear.

Yeah, yeah. I know. I'm dead. Nothing can really hurt me. I'm about as hurt as I can get. But apparently those old human instincts are slow to die.

So there I was, standing in the middle of the store staring at the back door like a rabbit caught in the middle of the road when Stephen Davenport walked in. He, too, froze.

My shoulders slumped as I heaved a sigh of relief.

"You scared the hell out of me," I said. I moved back to the doorway between the display room and the workshop.

Davenport didn't move, but his eyes grew rounder. "Back at you," he said warily, his hand gripping the still-open door.

"I was looking for you," I said.

"Yeah?" He eased the door shut behind him. "Why?"

"I need your help," I said.

He leaned back against the door, his eyes still wary. "What are you?"

Not who. What.

"So you really did see that bit with the cars?"

"Yeah."

I sighed. "I'm dead."

He tilted his head and looked me up and down. "You don't look dead."

"Good," I said. "I think dead is probably a bad look on most people. Glad it's working out for me."

"You're awfully sarcastic for a dead person."

"I was a pretty sarcastic live person, too."

"I'm not sure that helps any," he said.

"Maybe it would be easier to think of me as a ghost."

"No, not really," he said, shaking his head. He clasped his hands in front of him and stayed plastered against the door.

"A helpful spirit?" I suggested.

"That might be a little better."

"At least you haven't peed yourself," I said, trying to sound encouraging.

He looked down at his crotch as if affirming the fact for himself. "At least," he finally agreed, looking back up at me.

"So see? It could be much worse."

He didn't answer.

I sighed. "Look. I'm not going to hurt you. I meant it the other day when I told you that I didn't believe Rick killed Molly. In fact, I know he didn't, because I was there. I just want to find evidence to prove Rick's innocence."

"You were there?"

"Yeah."

"When Molly died?"

"Yeah." My voice grew quiet.

"So why didn't you stop it?"

I looked at him for a moment, and then waved my hand up and down and back and forth, through the wall. "Not much power to move stuff," I said.

All the blood drained from his face and he slumped a little against the door.

"Oh, hell," I said. "Don't faint on me, dammit. I told you I was a ghost."

"I don't think I really believed it," he whispered hoarsely.

"Why don't you have a seat and let's talk about this, okay?"

He nodded weakly and sank down onto the nearest bench.

"I tried to stop it," I said. "I really did. But they couldn't see me, so the killer just . . . killed her." I shook my head, trying to clear the images of Molly dead in the bathtub. "So now all I can do is get the right guy arrested."

"And you think I can help?" Stephen asked.

"You're one of the few people who can actually see

me. And you care about what happens to Rick. So yes, I'm hoping that you'll help me."

He stared down at his hands for a moment.

"Why isn't Molly's ghost here?"

I shrugged. "I don't know. I haven't seen any other ghosts since the day I died. But it hasn't been all that long, so maybe they're just not speaking to me yet."

"Why can I see you when other people can't?"

"I don't know. There's a lot I don't know. But if you'll help, I promise I'll tell you if I figure any of it out." I stood completely still, waiting for his answer, hoping I wouldn't have to go search for yet another person who could see me.

He looked back down, and then finally nodded. "Okay. I'll help."

*   *   *   *

We went back to Ashara's in Stephen's car.

"Can't you just pop over there or something?" he asked.

"Why does everyone keep expecting me to voluntarily teleport myself around?" I threw my hands up in the air and stared up at the sky as if waiting for an answer from heaven. *As if heaven has any part in my afterlife*, I thought, shaking my head and slipping into Stephen's little Honda through the closed door.

"You know," he said as he opened the driver's side door and climbed in, "that's a little creepy."

"Can't very well open the door," I said. "Come on, let's go. I want to get started on all of this."

Ashara was sitting at her computer when I moved into her house, calling out "I'm here! It's Callie!" to keep from startling her.

"Hey," she said without getting up from the computer. "I think I've got something."

"Me, too," I said. "I need you to unlock the front door to let him in."

She looked up at that. "You got him to come over here

already?"

"Yep, already. He's waiting on the porch."

When Ashara opened the door, she and Stephen just stared at each other for a long, silent moment.

"Um. Hi," he finally said.

"Oh. Yeah. Hi," she replied, almost stumbling over her own feet to move out of the way. "Come in, please."

I stood behind her. "Stephen Davenport, this is Ashara Jones. Ashara, Stephen."

Stephen stepped inside and stood awkwardly in the living room as Ashara shut the door. By the time she turned around, though, she had regained some of her usual composure. "Could I get you something to drink?"

"Water would be nice," he said.

Ashara nodded and headed for the kitchen.

"Have a seat," I offered, gesturing around at the couch. Stephen nodded and sat down at one end, hand tapping restlessly at the armrest.

"So," Ashara said as she came back into the room and handed him a glass of ice water. "I take it Callie told you what's going on?"

"Sort of," Stephen said.

I nodded. "I caught him up on everything on the way over here."

"I'm still a little fuzzy on some of the details," Stephen said. "Like how you two got involved in all this, for one thing. And why you," he nodded toward me, "can't go anywhere without Ashara's grandmother."

"Yeah, well," I said. "I'm a little fuzzy on that one myself."

"But," Stephen added, "I'm ready to help if it means getting Rick out of trouble."

"Good," said Ashara. She nodded approvingly. *When did she get so gung-ho about this*? I wondered. "I've got some questions for you, then."

Stephen nodded.

"The night that Callie and I went into the shop, the guy who came in after us had a key. So who all has keys to the shop?" she asked.

I stared at her with my mouth hanging open. I couldn't believe I hadn't even bothered to think of that question.

"Well," said Stephen, "everybody who works there, for a start."

"Does a Clifford Howard work there?"

Stephen shook his head.

"How do you know that's the guy's first name?" I asked Ashara.

"Maw-Maw got it out of him when she started asking him about his family the other day."

Of course she had.

"And this Clifford Howard guy is the one who killed Molly?" Stephen asked.

I nodded.

"So why don't you just go to the police about it now that you know his name?" Stephen asked.

Ashara and I stared at each other in exasperation. "Because," she said slowly, "the only reason we know he did it is that Callie saw him do it. And the cops probably aren't going to take a ghost's word for it."

Stephen stared at me. "Oh. Yeah. I guess I forgot that part for a minute."

"Good," I said briskly. "The more you think of me as a real person, the happier we'll all be."

"So this guy had a key to the shop," Stephen said musingly.

"Yeah. He walked right in, stood over Jeffrey McClatchey's desk, and picked something up. Something small. He put it into his pocket and left."

"So that's why you came back the other day?" Stephen asked me.

"Yeah. I wanted to see what I could figure out. Have you heard anything else about the piano wire the police picked up out of the trash?"

"No. Not that they'd tell me. But I do know that Rick's been charged and there's some sort of preliminary hearing next Monday. For bail or something."

"Does Rick have enough money to bail himself out?" Ashara asked.

Stephen shrugged. "I don't even know if he's got enough money for a good lawyer. It seemed like everything he made went back into that business. Molly's job was the one that paid for the house and stuff. At least, that was the sense I got of it."

I nodded. I hadn't spent all those evenings at the McClatchey's house without learning a little bit about them.

"So have you talked to Rick since he got arrested?"

Stephen shook his head. "No. I keep thinking I ought to go visit him, but I can't figure out what I'd say to him. 'Dude. Sorry your wife's dead and you're in jail.' Doesn't seem very comforting, really."

"Okay," I said. "I think we should write down everything we know. And by 'we,' I mean one of y'all, since I can't hold a pen very well anymore."

Ashara nodded, stood up, and came back with writing supplies.

"Okay," I said. "You said you had something, Ashara?"

"Yeah. I found a couple of possibilities for that phone number you gave me. Both local numbers, but I didn't recognize the names."

"Write them down anyway."

She used the number as a sort of heading and under the number, she wrote "David Evans and Allison Brown," along with the full telephone number connected to them.

"Recognize either of those people?" I asked Stephen. He shook his head.

The next heading was "Key," and under that, Ashara wrote the day and time of Clifford Howard's meeting with the person he'd talked to on the phone.

"What else?" she asked.

"Evidence," I said.

She wrote down the heading. "What do we have?"

"Well," I said, "the police have a drop of Howard's blood, but they clearly haven't figured out its significance yet. They've got the piano wire that killed Molly and the piano wire that was in Jeffrey's trash can, but we don't know if those things will even match up."

"The rumor at the shop is that part of the problem is Rick's alibi. He headed home from his conference early enough that it shouldn't have taken him that long to get home. He says he stopped to get something to eat, but Molly was apparently in the middle of cooking dinner when she was attacked. So the police don't believe him when he says he wasn't there."

"But we know for sure that he wasn't. So he probably really did stop to eat," Ashara said.

I nodded. "Molly might have been planning to surprise him. It's the sort of thing she would have been likely to do."

"Is that everything?" Ashara asked.

"I think we ought to have a special category listing everything else we know about Howard," I said.

"Okay." She wrote it down, then listed what we knew: killer, has key to shop, has small key, took something from Jeffrey's desk, has meeting tomorrow, called phone number to set up meeting.

"Didn't you say that there was another number on a sheet of paper?" Ashara asked.

"Oh. Yeah." I struggled for a moment to remember the number, and then gave it to her. "203. Why? Do you have some idea what it might be?"

She shook her head. "I keep thinking that I ought to know what it is, but I can't remember." She shook her head again. "I think I need to get some sleep. Maybe it'll come to me by morning."

I stood up. "Okay, then. We'll get Maw-Maw tomorrow and see if we can follow this guy."

Ashara nodded. "You be damned careful with my grandmother, though. If you get her hurt, I'll kill you."

"Too late," I said cheerfully. "Seriously. We'll stay far enough back that he won't even know we're following him. Right, Stephen?"

"Right." He nodded, but he didn't seem as delighted with the plan as I was. But at least he was on board.

"Okay, then. I'll see y'all tomorrow." I wafted out through the door, and then waited for Stephen to follow me. It took a long moment, but finally the door opened and he stepped out.

"What took so long?" I asked.

"Ashara had to explain to me what she would do to me if her grandmother got into any sort of trouble." His voice sounded subdued.

"Ah. Yeah. I can see how that would take a while."

Chapter Eleven

We picked Maw-Maw up at 10:30 the next morning. She was already sitting on the swing on her front porch waiting for us. She stared at Stephen through her thick glasses as we walked up the sidewalk.

"Miss Adelaide," I said, "this is Stephen Davenport. Stephen, this is Adelaide Thompkins."

"Nice to meet you, ma'am," he said.

She surveyed him up and down, peering at him intently. "Oh, well," she said. "I guess he'll do."

Stephen and I exchanged startled glances.

"Miss Adelaide," I said, "Stephen's here to help us out." He offered his arm to help her to her feet. "I guess he is at that," she said, picking up her cane and hobbling down the steps. She leaned heavily on his arm.

I hovered nearby while Stephen got Maw-Maw settled into the car.

"Tell me again why she has to go with us," he said as he moved around to his side of the car.

"Because I can't leave town without her," I said. "Kind of like American Express, only worse."

I slid into the back seat.

"So," said Maw-Maw, "how we going to do this?"

"You're going to take me out of town, then wait by the end of the road. Just wait until Howard drives by, and then follow him."

I felt that same rubber-bandy belly-button sensation I'd had before when we passed by the city limits sign, but it wasn't quite as strong as it had been the first time.

The morning was sunny and bright--not the sort of day one expects to spend chasing murderers to their secret meetings. Those sorts of days ought to be dank and dark, shrouded in fog.

Then again, the dead ought to spend their afterlives someplace other than Alabama. So much for "ought."

Anyway, the plan went . . . well, as planned. Stephen and Maw-Maw pulled off to the side of the road, hidden from the old dirt road by the trees, but still able to see its intersection with the highway.

I flitted off to Howard's house, hoping that we'd gotten there early enough.

Barely, I thought, as I slipped into the passenger seat of the white SUV. We jounced along in silence for a while--not surprising, since Howard couldn't see me. As we pulled out onto the highway, I craned my neck to see if Stephen and Maw-Maw were following us.

For a second I thought they'd missed the car, but then Stephen pulled out onto the highway after two other cars had passed, leaving enough space between him and the SUV to keep Howard from suspecting he was being followed.

We drove back into town.

Great, I thought. *I didn't need Maw-Maw after all. I could have just waited on the side of the road. Dammit.*

We drove through the center of town, past the statue of the general. I waved at it cheerily; suddenly glad to know that at least I wasn't tied to it any more. Rather to my surprise, a child crossing the street with his mother waved back at me. I smiled and he smiled back.

I had forgotten how nice it could be just to be seen and acknowledged--with something other than pants-peeing, anyway.

The little boy distracted me enough that I was surprised when we pulled up in front of the bank.

Ashara's bank.

Howard parked the SUV and got out, heading into the white building.

A moment later, Stephen and Maw-Maw pulled up, too. They parked several spots down from Howard, but the parking lot only had four other cars in it. They weren't exactly inconspicuous.

Maw-Maw rolled down her window. "What now?" she

asked.

"I think you'd better go home," I said. "I'll come get you if I need you."

"Nope," the old woman said. "No way."

"Then at least go park in some other parking lot," I said to Stephen. "This guy knows who Miss Adelaide is."

Stephen nodded and put the car into gear.

I moved into the bank as they pulled out of the parking lot. At first glance, I couldn't see Howard, and for a moment I panicked. Then I realized that he was sitting down at one of the desks scattered around the room, a plump blonde woman sitting across from him entering information into a computer. Howard hunched over a form, laboriously filling it out.

I slipped across the room and stared at it over his shoulder.

An application for a checking account.

This wasn't making any sense at all.

Or at least, it wasn't until I saw Jeffrey McClatchey walk in, a battered brown suitcase in his hand.

He and Howard made eye contact, then nodded slightly, acknowledging one another. In a small town like Abramsville, it would be seen as a polite gesture--if anyone noticed at all. Given what I knew, the nods took on more significance. McClatchey stood back, waiting to talk to the same woman Howard was with.

The woman behind the desk stood up and handed Howard a stack of temporary checks. "There you go, Mr. Johnson. All set. We're glad to welcome you to our bank." She smiled and they shook hands.

Mr. Johnson? I thought. *What the hell?*

Then Howard put his hand into his pocket, casually, before turning around.

And then pulled it back out again as he greeted Jeffrey McClatchey. The two men shook hands, and I saw the glint of the tiny key being passed from Howard to McClatchey. Howard walked toward the back of the bank, then stopped and turned around. "Excuse me," he said to the woman he'd just left, "but is there a restroom I could use?"

"Certainly," she said, and pointed him in the right direction. "Now," she said, turning back to McClatchey, "you said you'd like to get into a safe deposit box?"

Of course. That was what Ashara had been trying to put together the night before. The number on the slip of paper Howard had pulled out of his desk the other night was a safe deposit box number. And this was the key to a very important one.

Damn.

I hesitated for an instant, trying to decide what I should do: try to get to the safe deposit box first or warn Ashara that our two prime murder suspects were in her bank.

People, I thought. *People are more important than anything else.*

I moved as swiftly as I could to the drive-through tellers' windows.

"Ashara," I hissed from behind her.

She jumped a little, but to her credit, she didn't scream. Or even turn around. She just muttered "Huh?" under her breath.

"Howard is here. And so is Rick McClatchey's brother. They're here in the bank. Something weird is up--and McClatchey has that key and is going to use it to get into a safe deposit box."

Ashara's head tilted to one side and she nodded slightly.

"I'm going to go keep an eye on them. I'll be back in a little bit," I said. She nodded again as if in time to some inner song. *If she keeps doing that, someday her colleagues are going to decide she is crazy,* I thought.

I raced to the safe deposit room, hoping to beat them there and open number 203 for myself. After all, I knew I could.

If only I'd figured it out sooner, I thought in a silent

wail. I could have opened the box and seen what was in it.

I didn't have time, of course. If I'd popped the box open, both McClatchey and the bank officer would have noticed. I stood in the middle of the room, muttering a steady stream of curses.

Once the two got into the safe deposit room, the woman inserted her key and turned it, then showed McClatchey how to use his key to open the box. She also showed him how to close his box once he was done looking through it. She pulled the box out for him, had him sign some sort of sheet, and then left the room. "Just let me know when you're done," she said.

"Thanks, ma'am," he said, and opened up the box. I peered over his shoulder.

It was full of cash. Stuffed to the brim. I saw twenties and hundreds, and maybe even an old thousand dollar bill, though I couldn't have sworn to it.

McClatchey took the money and stuffed it into his briefcase, then put the safe deposit box back and locked it.

He headed out of the safe room, and I sped out in front of him. I needed to tell Maw-Maw and Stephen to follow us again.

I hadn't gotten far, though, when I saw Ashara coming out of the tellers' restroom. At the same moment, Howard stepped out of the men's room. He looked up and he and McClatchey nodded at one another again, just the barest of nods. McClatchey stopped by the bank officer's desk to let her know he was done, and then headed out the front door.

Meanwhile, Ashara's face was down and she wasn't watching where she was going. She smoothed her skirt down and looked up just in time to avoid running into Howard.

They locked eyes.

No, I thought. *No. Oh no, oh no, oh no.*

"Don't say his name!" I shouted at Ashara. "Pretend you don't recognize him!"

Startled, she glanced in my direction. At empty air, as

far as anyone else in the bank could tell.

"Excuse me," she said to Howard, brushing past him. "Sorry about that."

Howard didn't say anything, but he gave Ashara a long, hard stare as she walked back toward the back of the bank and her teller's window. Then he moved slowly toward the entrance.

Once I was sure Ashara was once again safely behind bullet-proof glass, I rushed out into the parking lot and looked around frantically. McClatchey was just starting up the engine on his Ford pickup truck and Howard had his SUV in gear. I searched wildly for Stephen and Maw-Maw.

I finally spotted them in the parking lot of the McDonald's across the street.

"Follow us!" I shouted, waving my arms and jumping into the passenger seat of McClatchey's car. Stephen looked startled, but he nodded and started up his own car again.

I glanced at the truck's clock. 11:30. If he was the one meeting up with Howard, they couldn't be going very far for their noon meeting.

I was right. We pulled up to Ira's, the town's only non-chain burger joint--a tiny place that served homemade burgers and fries and made, according to the sign, the best milkshakes in town.

McClatchey pulled into a space in the very back of the parking lot and hauled the briefcase up into the middle of the passenger seat.

Which meant, of course, that he hauled it up into the middle of me. And then he opened it and started sorting through the cash, which meant that his hands were moving in and out of my thighs. Yuck. I slipped into the back seat and leaned over to watch.

First he sorted the money into piles by denomination. I'd been right. There were several thousand-dollar bills in the case. I was surprised, as I was pretty certain that the government had quit making thousand-dollar bills a long time ago--years and years. That meant this money was old. Some of it, at least.

The sight of the big bills threw me off, and I forgot to keep count with McClatchey. Still, it was a lot. Maybe in the tens of thousands of dollars? Thirty? Forty?

Yeah, I know. Thirty or forty thousand dollars isn't really all that much, not even enough to buy a house with. But if I were to bet on it, I'd bet that people have killed for less. And I was guessing that all this money had something to do with Molly McClatchey's death.

Once McClatchey had counted it all, he split it in half. Every so often he'd look up to make sure that no one could see what he was doing in the passenger seat. Half of the bills went back into the briefcase. The other half went into an old plastic grocery sack that he pulled out from under the seat.

After he'd split the money, he stared at the briefcase for a long moment. Then he reached in, grabbed a handful of bills, and shoved them into the grocery bag.

He smiled a little and nodded, then snapped the briefcase closed. The grocery bag full of cash he shoved back under the passenger seat.

I'd been so intent on watching what McClatchey was doing that I'd forgotten to look for Stephen and Maw-Maw. I was going to have to get better at paying attention to more than one thing at a time if I hoped to save Rick McClatchey.

This business was getting complicated.

But not nearly as complicated as it was about to get, I realized as I floated into the burger joint behind Howard.

Stephen and Maw-Maw were seated in a booth in the back, munching on hamburgers.

"What are you doing here?" I hissed at them. I slid into the booth next to Maw-Maw, both to get a clear view of the restaurant and in the hopes that my proximity might keep her quiet.

No such luck.

"Me and this nice boy here are just out for some

lunch," she said at her normal volume.

The couple in the booth next to us smiled and nodded, unsure whether Maw-Maw was talking to them or just slightly demented.

"I couldn't stop her," Stephen murmured to me.

I shook my head and watched McClatchey order at the front counter. He slid into one of the bright orange booths toward the front of the restaurant, near the windows.

Stephen's back was to the front of the room. He started to turn around to see what had caught my attention, but I shook my head at him sharply.

"Get down," I whispered to him. He slouched down in the booth.

A few moments later, McClatchey sat up a little straighter. So did I, craning my neck to see what he had seen.

The door opened and in walked Howard.

"Now, Miss Adelaide," I said. "Don't you answer me. I need you to stay very, very quiet. I don't want the man who just walked in to see you. He's already seen you once and he's nervous. So you just finish your burger and we'll wait until he leaves."

Maw-Maw peered at me through her thick glasses.

"Well. You don't have to talk to me like I'm stupid, you know," she said. Aloud.

Stephen smiled apologetically at the couple in the next booth.

"No ma'am," he said. "I know you're not."

I sighed. This was a disaster. At least McClatchey wasn't paying any attention to the other diners. He stared out the window, absently chewing the burger he'd ordered.

Maw-Maw ate her burger in a huff, glaring at me now and again but saying nothing further.

Howard stood to the side of the counter until his order was ready. Then brought it out into the dining room on a little orange tray.

And sat down right behind McClatchey, their backs to

one another in the booth.

The men never acknowledged one another. But McClatchey, I realized, had placed the briefcase on the floor beside his booth. And now, ever so slowly, never looking up from his lunch, he curled his leg around the side of the booth and nudged the briefcase with his foot until it was sitting beside Clifford Howard's booth.

Then McClatchey got up to leave. Casually, Howard reached down and picked up the briefcase, placing it beside him on the booth seat.

And in the entire crowded restaurant, I was the only one who saw it happen.

At least, that's what I thought, until I saw Maw-Maw staring at Howard intently, then looking back and forth between the two men.

Howard finished his burger, too, and followed McClatchey out the door. He made it all the way to the front entrance before he felt the weight of Maw-Maw's stare. For an instant, I thought we were safe. But then Howard turned back and surveyed the restaurant one last time.

Just one last time. Just long enough to catch Maw-Maw's stare.

Again, as with Ashara, Howard froze and stared intently.

"Look down," I said to Maw-Maw. "Look at your food. Try to look like you can't really see anything."

And for once, wonder of wonders, she did what I told her to. Without comment.

After what seemed like half an hour but was probably only a few seconds, Howard left the restaurant, the glass door swinging shut behind him.

"Now," I said to Stephen. "While he's getting into his car. Look outside. Not Howard. The other one."

Stephen sat up and spun around in his seat. With a gasp, he slumped back into his original hiding position.

"That's Rick's brother," he hissed.

I nodded. "And just wait until you hear the rest of it," I said.

Maw-Maw started to scoot out of her seat.

"Don't anybody move," I said to Maw-Maw and Stephen. "We're not out of trouble yet." Maw-Maw stopped fussing and they both nodded, subdued. Stephen sank even further into his seat.

The couple next to us finished their burgers and left, smiling at Maw-Maw as if she were perhaps a little senile. Maw-Maw returned their smile with a snarl.

"I ain't stupid," she said to them.

The woman of the pair drew herself up as if to say something, but her husband grabbed her arm and hurried her out of the restaurant.

We continued to sit in silence long after Stephen and Maw-Maw had both finished eating.

Chapter Twelve

"No fucking way," Stephen said. We were seated in Maw-Maw's living room discussing the events of the day. Ashara hadn't come home from work yet, but the others hadn't been willing to wait for her; they wanted me to tell them everything I'd seen.

"Watch your language, young man," Maw-Maw said, but her voice was distracted. "You're positive that briefcase was full of money?" she asked me.

"Absolutely. A lot of money. And some of it looked old."

"Hmm." Maw-Maw patted her bottom lip as she pondered.

"I just don't believe that Jeff would have anything to do with something that horrible," Stephen said. "I've worked with the guy for four years now. He's a nice guy."

"Right. A nice guy who gives money to the man who cut Molly McClatchey into bite-size chunks," I said.

Stephen shook his head. "I'm sorry. I know it looks horrible. You're probably right. I'm just having a hard time believing it. I mean, I've gone out for beers with the guy after work, you know? You just never think someone you know could do something like that."

I nodded, and wished for a moment that I could touch his shoulder or something. The moment passed, though. He needed to face reality more than he needed to be comforted.

"Okay," I said. "That's one more thing that we can add to the list of things we know."

"What's that?" Ashara asked, coming in through the front door.

I repeated the morning's events for her.

"Damn, girl," said Ashara on a slow breath. She shook her head.

"Ashara," her grandmother said warningly.

"I know, I know. Watch my mouth. But you gotta

admit, Maw-Maw, that one might be worth a curse word or two."

Maw-Maw laughed. "Maybe so," she acknowledged.

"Okay, then," Stephen said. "What next?"

I shook my head. "I'm not sure."

"I am," Ashara said. She smiled smugly.

We all stared at her, waiting.

"Well?" I finally demanded. "Tell us."

"Next, we need to find out who all is on the signature card for that safe deposit box--there's no way Jeffrey McClatchey could have gotten into it otherwise. But I'm guessing that money wasn't his to begin with."

"Of course," I said, stunned that I hadn't thought of it myself. "He might be on the card, but the money isn't really his. Why would he have had to have Howard steal the key from Rick otherwise?"

"And you can do that--get into those records and find out who had access to the box?" Stephen asked her.

She nodded. "I think so. It's not the sort of thing I usually have to look up, but I know how to do it."

"You realize that looking up that information is probably illegal on several levels, don't you?" I asked.

"Not as illegal as having some woman cut up and left in the bathtub," Maw-Maw said. "No. You go get that information for us, Ashara. Just don't get caught."

"No, ma'am," said Ashara. "I won't."

*   *   *   *

"So are you at all worried about the fact that that Howard guy saw both of them?" Stephen asked me as we left Maw-Maw's house. Ashara had stayed behind; she said she wanted to make sure Maw-Maw had dinner before Ashara left for her own house that night.

"Terrified," I answered.

"Yeah. Me, too."

"If I could think of any way to keep them safe, I would," I said.

Stephen nodded. "I suppose I could keep watch," he said doubtfully.

I shook my head. "You're only one person and you have to sleep at some point. No. I don't think Howard is worried enough to do anything yet. And all he knows for sure about how to find them again is that Ashara works at the bank. I think she's probably safe there."

Stephen nodded. "You're right. I'm sure they're both safe in their own homes, too. But I'm still worried."

I nodded in agreement. We parted ways at his car. "Sure you don't want a ride somewhere?" he asked, rolling down the window and leaning out from behind the steering wheel.

"Certain," I said. "I'm a ghost, remember? I don't need a car anymore."

He smiled wanly and put the car into gear.

"Come find me at work tomorrow if you learn anything new," he said.

I nodded. "And if Jeffrey McClatchey comes in, try to act normal," I said.

Stephen shuddered. "I'll try. But he hasn't been in since Molly's death."

"Good," I said. "Maybe you won't ever have to see him at work again."

I waved at him as he pulled away from the driveway.

I'd lied. Sort of, anyway. I didn't need a ride from Stephen, but it wasn't because I could fly anywhere I needed to go. It was because I had no plans to go anywhere. Unlike the living, I didn't need sleep. As long as I didn't expend too much energy on trying to have some effect on the physical world, I could go for days without doing my little floaty-resting thing.

So I was going to spend the night moving back and forth between Ashara's and Maw-Maw's. Just to be sure.

I really hadn't liked the way Howard had stared at them.

Nothing happened that night. I could have saved myself a lot of trouble, flitting back and forth from one house to the other. But it made me feel better to know that they were safe. And what else was I going to do? Being dead and awake when everyone else is sleeping is super double extra boring. It's like the worst case of insomnia you've ever had times roughly seventy-two. It's that bad.

So yeah. Watching out for Ashara and Maw-Maw gave me something to do. Not that I had any idea what I could have done if Howard had shown up.

I needed to start practicing throwing things, I decided. Being a poltergeist might come in handy.

Anyway, I quit floating back and forth once the sun rose. By the time Ashara got to work, I was already in the teller's booth.

"Hi!" I said brightly.

She ignored me. Probably the wise thing to do, since her co-worker Ann was already there.

"So," I said. "When are you going to look up the safe deposit box number?"

She shook her head.

"That means not now, doesn't it?"

She nodded slightly.

"You want me to go away now?"

She nodded again, this time more emphatically.

"Okay, I said, "but I'm going to check in later. Repeatedly. So you might want to look it up sooner rather than later."

Ashara sighed.

I grinned and floated out through the bullet-proof window, waving.

"Hey," I said, sticking my head back into the room through the glass. "Not ghost proof!"

Ashara sighed deeply and closed her eyes for a moment.

"You okay?" Ann asked from the other teller's station.

I grinned even wider and pulled back out of the window.

My grin faded when I moved around to the side of the bank and saw Howard standing in the parking lot examining cars.

It didn't take him long to find Ashara's. I watched him as he wrote down the license plate number. Then he got into his SUV and started the engine.

I froze, torn between warning Ashara and trying to find out what Howard might do with the information.

At the last minute, I jumped up and into the back of the SUV. As long as Howard was leaving the bank, Ashara was in no immediate danger. And we needed to know what he might do now that he had a way to find out who she was.

I slipped into the back seat from the cargo space, hoping that Howard wouldn't leave the city limits.

He didn't. He went to the local library first. Which had internet access, of course. And there he looked up Ashara's license plate number, just as we had looked up his.

Of course, unlike Howard, Ashara's license plate matched up with her name and address.

Dammit.

My only consolation was that he hadn't comparison shopped as Ashara had. He'd paid $99.99 for the information.

Then again, he had a briefcase full of cash, probably his ill-gotten gain from his murder of Molly McClatchey. He could afford it. *The son of a bitch*, I thought as I stared over his shoulder.

He reached for a sheet of paper and pen to copy down the address. And that's when I remembered that I could screw with electronics.

I know. I probably should have done something before he looked up the information. What can I say? I'm still getting used to being dead.

Anyway, I did manage to short out the computer--put

my palm on top of the casing and totally crashed it--just before he wrote down her name and address. A small victory, but his muttered curse made me smile.

By the time I was done with him, he was cursing out loud. Every time he tried to turn on a computer, it crashed. He moved from machine to machine until all three of the small library's terminals showed nothing but blank blue screens.

A small Asian librarian came hustling over as Howard's curses got louder.

"Can I help you?" she asked.

"Yeah," he said. "You can turn on one of these goddamned machines."

She put her finger to her lips. "Of course, of course. Shh."

She reached behind the row of monitors and flicked the switch on the surge protectors. All three computers booted up.

"There you go, sir," she said in an exaggerated whisper. "All set."

"Thanks," Howard said gruffly. Then he sat down to pull up the information again. I let him get as far as the login page for the website he needed before sending a surge of electricity through the machine.

It rebooted.

Howard cursed.

The fourth time this happened--on the third machine-- Howard stood up and slammed his hand down onto the monitor. The librarian looked up in alarm.

"Fuck it," Howard muttered. I followed him as he left the library, hoping that he had gotten frustrated enough to forget Ashara's information, since he hadn't written it down.

That was my hope, anyway.

I was only half right. We got into his SUV and drove straight to Ashara's street. But once we were there, he drove up and down it, peering intently at each house, as if he could somehow divine which one belonged to Ashara.

Eventually he gave up--with another loud curse--and

headed out of town. I stayed with him as long as I could just in case he made a detour before heading home. But he didn't, and as we passed the city limits sign, I felt the rubber-band tug at my stomach. With a *pop!* I stood in the middle of Maw-Maw's living room. Maw-Maw sat in her usual spot in the chair.

She stared up at me through her glasses, unperturbed.

"Well hello, Callie dear," she said.

"Hi, Miss Adelaide," I said. I leaned in close to her and brushed a kiss near her cheek. She reached up and patted my cheek, ignoring the fact that her hand went halfway through my face.

"I can't stay right now, Miss Adelaide," I said. "I need to go talk to Ashara. But I'll be back in just a little bit."

"Okay, honey," she said. "You just come on back here whenever you're ready."

I sped over to the bank as quickly as I could, eschewing street-level travel and skimming across the tops of houses. Once I got there, I slipped into the tellers' booth.

Ashara took one look at my face and turned to her colleague. "I'm going to take a quick bathroom break, okay?"

"No problem," Ann replied.

I followed Ashara into the bathroom, talking the whole time.

"So now he knows what street you live on and what car you drive. All he'd have to do is wait on your street and he'd be able to find out where you live."

Ashara leaned against the closed door of the two-stall restroom.

"Damn," she said. "That's not good."

"And that's an understatement," I agreed.

She sighed. "Okay, then. I'll stay with Maw-Maw until we get this all sorted out."

I nodded. "Good idea."

She shook her head. "But there are things I'll eventually need to get from my house. I keep a couple of changes of clothes at Maw-Maw's, but not enough to get me through more than a few days at work."

"We'll figure something out," I promised. "I just don't want you to go back over there today."

"Okay." She nodded and put her hand on the door handle.

"And put your car inside her garage. Don't just leave it out; he knows what it looks like and this is a small town."

"Okay, okay," she said. "I've got to get back to work now."

"Wait," I said. "Have you had a chance to look up that safe deposit box yet?"

"Not yet. But I can do it when Ann takes her lunch break."

I nodded. "And hey--don't leave work tonight until I'm sure the coast is clear. I don't want Howard following you to your grandmother's."

Ashara slumped against the door. "Oh, God. I never thought of that."

"Don't worry about it now," I said. "Just go back into work. I'll go see what I can figure out."

I left the bank and headed straight for Rick McClatchey's shop. I found Stephen in the back replacing the keys on a saxophone.

"Hey," he said quietly, looking up from placing some arcane piece of metal into a C-clamp to hold it together while the glue dried.

At the sound of his voice, the older woman looked up from her bench. "Yes?" she said.

"Nothing," Stephen said. "I need a break. I'm going to walk around the block or something. I'll be back in a few minutes."

The woman nodded and bent back over her task-- something involving tiny pieces of metal and a miniature soldering iron.

I told him what I'd seen that morning as we moved around the downtown square.

"That sucks," he said, stopping to stare at the display in the window of Felix's Pharmacy.

"Sure does," I agreed. "And it worries me."

He nodded. "I think it might be time to go see Rick," he said.

"Can we do that?" I asked.

"Well, they've moved him to Birmingham, so Maw-Maw will have to go with us if you want in on the interview."

"Birmingham?"

Stephen nodded. "Haven't you been watching the news? Or reading a newspaper?"

"Um. No. Can't turn the pages all that easily," I said.

"Oh." Stephen stared at me for a minute. "I forgot."

"Well," I said, "you might as well tell me."

"The Abramsville police department decided that they didn't have a secure enough facility for such a dangerous criminal." His voice sounded sour. "All they've really got is a two-cell jail, and both of those are usually taken up with drunks. So they've moved Rick to a jail in Birmingham."

"Jail? Not prison?"

"No. I think they're waiting for a conviction before putting him in with the really hardened criminals. Not that the media's waiting for a trial. They've already decided he's guilty. Even if they do say 'alleged killer'." He shook his head.

"Anyway," he said. "If you can't leave town without Ashara's grandmother, then she has to go with us."

I chewed on my lower lip, then nodded. "Yeah. I'm sure she'll be thrilled to go. Ashara won't be so happy with us, but she'll get over it."

"Hey," said Stephen suddenly, staring at my face. "Can you feel that?"

"Feel what?"

"When you chew on your lip like that. Can you feel it?"

I thought about it. "I guess so. I mean, it's just a habit."

"So you feel like you have a body?"

Now it was my turn to stare at him. "Yes. I feel like I have a body. It's just that if I'm not concentrating really hard, it feels like the rest of the world isn't . . . I don't know. Real. Solid."

I moved past the window display and headed back to Rick's shop. "Mostly I don't think about it."

Stephen nodded, following me. "Makes sense. I mean, most of us don't really think about our own bodies all that much. Not unless they're bothering us."

"Can we quit talking about this?" I said. "It's kind of creeping me out."

"Hey," said Stephen. "You're the ghost here. If anyone should be creeped out, it's me."

I sighed. "Just go back to work and tell them whatever you need to tell them. Then come pick me up at Maw-Maw's."

Stephen grinned, his usual good humor returning. "Yes, ma'am, Ms. Ghost." He saluted me and loped back across the square. I watched his back as he departed. His blond curls ruffled in the slight breeze.

Kind of cute, I thought, then shook my head. Way too alive for me. Or maybe I was way too dead for him. Either way, it didn't matter; his cuteness didn't--couldn't--concern me.

I sighed. I'd spent a lot of time avoiding thinking about all the things I'd never get to do again. Eat. Sleep. Touch someone. Have sex. Ever.

God. This is depressing, I thought. Maybe going to visit a man wrongly accused of butchering his wife would be just the thing to cheer me up. I smiled grimly and headed back to the bank to let Ashara know the plan.

Ashara didn't approve, but since Ann was in the teller's booth with her, all she could do was stare at me with huge eyes and clenched jaw and shake her head.

"Oh," I said as I moved toward the exit, "and don't worry about being followed to Maw-Maw's tonight. Just head over there after work today. I have a plan."

I could hear her exasperated sigh as I ducked out through the bank.

*   *   *   *

"Okay," I said as Stephen, Maw-Maw, and I pulled out onto the highway. "I want you to pull over near Howard's place. I have something I need to do before we go to Birmingham."

"What you going to do?" Maw-Maw asked interestedly.

"I'll tell you if it works."

Maw-Maw looked at me suspiciously, then turned back around to face the front of the car. "Fine. You just keep your white ghost lady secrets."

I laughed. "It's not a secret, Miss Adelaide. I'll tell you all about it after it's done. And you can just quit calling me 'white ghost lady.' Don't think I don't know you only say that when you're irritated."

"Ooh," said Maw-Maw, "now you're Miss Uppity White Ghost Lady."

I laughed again, and this time Maw-Maw cackled with me.

Stephen pulled over at the entrance to the dirt road that led to Howard's place. As swiftly as I could, I flitted to Howard's house. I didn't move into the air until I was out of sight of the car, though. For some reason I was uncomfortable with the idea of Stephen and Maw-Maw seeing me float above the ground.

I was glad to see that Howard's SUV was in its accustomed parking spot. I stood over the hood and closed my eyes--for some reason, that seemed to help me concentrate better.

And then, much like I had with the computers the night before, I put my hand on the hood, thinking of energy running through wires, overloading them, shorting them out.

I felt a snap and a sort of sizzle, and then smelled the

faint sulfurous, ozone smell of fried wires.

I smiled. Beautiful. I'd be surprised if he could start that engine ever again. Not without some serious mechanical work on it and certainly not before we made it to Birmingham and back that day.

Howard would not be following Ashara anywhere today.

Maw-Maw cackled wildly and clapped her hands in delight when I got back to the car and told them what I'd done.

"Perfect," Stephen said. "And remind me never to piss you off. It's all I can do to keep this old heap running as it is."

They were holding Rick McClatchey in the Birmingham City Jail. I felt odd as we entered the building. I couldn't help remembering that this was the place where Martin Luther King, Jr. had written his open letter to the white clergymen who had called for "unity" against King's nonviolent protest. I could even almost remember part of the letter: "Individuals may see the moral light and give up their unjust posture; but groups are more immoral than individuals." Or something close to it, anyway. So entering this place gave me a chill, the kind that comes with knowing you've walked into someplace important.

But it wasn't just that. I had another kind of chill, too. I've always felt strangely guilty around police, even though I'm fairly law-abiding. Or rather, had been when I was alive. But I still get a kind of guilty feeling in the pit of my stomach whenever there are a lot of police officers in uniform around me.

Not that it mattered any more. There wasn't much left that a cop could do to me. Except maybe find my killer.

The waiting room was depressing. A tall black man in uniform sat at a desk behind bullet-proof glass and took down Stephen's and Maw-Maw's names, as well as the name of the prisoner they were there to see.

Then Stephen and Maw-Maw sat down in the hard plastic chairs of the waiting room. At one time the chairs had been a bright mix of primary colors, but now those colors had faded. The seats were worn smooth, almost white, and several of the chairs had blackened melted spots where someone had mashed out a cigarette at some point.

The room still smelled faintly of cigarette smoke, despite the plastic "No Smoking" signs screwed into the walls.

"This is awful," I said quietly to Stephen. He nodded without answering.

"I'm going into the back to see what I can see," I said. Again he nodded without answering.

The main door to the actual jail was controlled by the man behind the bullet-proof glass. I'd seen him push the button to buzz people through a couple of times since we'd been there.

I, on the other hand, did not need to be buzzed through. I could just float through.

That's what I thought, anyway. I'd gotten used to just sliding through doors and windows, not worrying about normal barriers.

Not that this door was any more of a barrier than most.

It just had an alarm on it.

And apparently I had enough energy, or something, to set this alarm off.

I was about halfway through the door when the screeching bell sounded. I jumped about two feet in the air-- quite literally--and came back down on the waiting room side of the door.

"Never mind," I said as I slid into the seat beside Stephen. "I think I'll wait."

"Probably a good idea," he agreed.

Maw-Maw hadn't said a word the whole time we'd been there. She just sat in her chair, her big black purse in her lap, her cane on top of her purse, and her arms folded on top of it all, and stared around the room.

The alarm caused no small amount of concern to the police officers in the building, but once it had been established that the door had never opened, they finally agreed that it must have been some kind of short. The man behind the counter made a phone call requesting a technician to come check out the door.

With all the excitement, it was almost an hour before we were called back to see Rick. Maw-Maw hadn't spoken in all that time.

I had expected that Stephen would have to talk to Rick through one of those telephone thingies like they always show on television--you know, where one person's on one side of the glass and the other person's behind the glass.

Here, though, the visitors were allowed to talk to the prisoners in a common visiting room. Medium-sized tables filled the room, and people in orange jumpsuits talked in hushed voices to people in street clothes. A few children ran around the room, playing with each other while their parents tried to calm them down. Uniformed officers stood scattered around the room.

The uniformed woman who had led us down the hall after calling Stephen's name placed us at a table. "McClatchey will be here in just a moment," she said in a pleasant but still serious voice.

Another uniformed officer led Rick into the room and over to our table.

Rick McClatchey looked like hell. And that was a generous assessment. He had big black circles under his eyes, which seemed to have sunk back into his skull. He had always been thin with a pale complexion, but now his face looked jaundiced and yellow. And his skin seemed to have sagged off his bones, as if he were too tired to even keep that much together. Looking at him, it was hard to believe that this change had taken place so quickly; Molly McClatchey had been dead less than a week.

"Hey, man," Stephen said in a quiet voice.

"Hey," said Rick. "What are you doing here?"

"I wanted to come see how you're doing," Stephen

said.

Rick's eyes flicked to Maw-Maw, but he didn't seem able to drag up the energy to ask who she was, even.

"Okay, I guess," he said. "As okay as I could be, anyway."

"I'm real sorry about Molly, Rick," Stephen said.

Rick's eyes met Stephen's and then flicked away. "Yeah. Me, too."

"I heard they denied bail," Stephen said.

"Yeah." Rick didn't look up. "Guess I'm stuck here until the trial." He laughed harshly.

"Ask him about his brother," I said.

Stephen flashed an irritated look at me.

"So what does your lawyer say?" he asked Rick.

Rick shook his head. "Not a whole lot just yet. He says they're working on getting the forensic evidence together." His voice trailed off.

"Yeah?" Stephen prompted.

"But he says it doesn't look good for me. He's already saying I should take a deal." He looked up at Stephen, and crossed his arms on the table, leaning over and staring into Stephen's face. The dullness fled his eyes, replaced by a burning intensity. "But I didn't do it, Stephen. I swear to you I didn't do it. I couldn't hurt Molly. Not ever." He dissolved into tears and put his head down on his crossed arms on the table.

Stephen awkwardly patted Rick's dark hair. "I know you didn't, man."

"Dammit, Stephen," I said. "Quit wasting time. Ask him about his brother and about Howard."

Stephen glared at me, and then took a deep breath. "Hey, Rick?"

Rick looked up, wiping his eyes angrily--but I sensed the anger had more to do with his own breakdown than with anything else. "What?" he asked.

"Do you know anyone with the last name Howard?"

Rick looked thoughtful for a second, and then shook his head. "Not that I can think of. Why?"

Stephen ignored the question and forged ahead with the harder one. "What about Jeffrey? Do you know of any reason he'd be angry with you or Molly?"

Rick looked stunned. "Jeff? No. He's been my biggest supporter in all this. He comes to see me nearly every day. He's the only one who believes I didn't do it."

"I'll just bet he does," I said sarcastically. Everyone ignored me.

"You don't think he had anything to do with it, do you?" Rick demanded. "Because he couldn't have, he's my brother. He knows I'm innocent."

"He's not the only one, Rick," Stephen said, again ignoring Rick's own questions. "We're all keeping the shop open, keeping it running for you. It'll be waiting for you when you beat this thing."

"Thanks." Rick's eyes welled up with tears again.

"No problem, man."

Suddenly Maw-Maw leaned forward. She had been so quiet for so long that I think we'd all almost forgotten she was there.

"Now you listen to me, young man," she said, pointing her finger at Rick and squinting at him through her glasses. She looked like an old witch, her gray hair sticking out from her bun in several directions, her fingers bony and gnarled. "You did not do this thing. We all know it. But you got to figure out who you can trust. And that brother of yours ain't no good. No good at all." She leaned back in her seat, satisfied at having said her piece.

Rick blinked at her, startled.

"Who are you?" he asked her, then stared at Stephen.

A uniformed officer walked up and loomed over our table. "Time's up, McClatchey," he said.

Rick sighed and stood up.

"Thanks for coming to see me," he said to Stephen. He

looked at Maw-Maw as if he'd like to say something more to her, but the officer led him away before he had a chance.

"So what do you think?" I asked after we were back on I-20 headed toward Abramsville.

"I think we don't really know more than we did before," Stephen said.

"That ain't true," Maw-Maw said.

Stephen and I both glanced at her, surprised.

"So what do we know now that we didn't know before?" I asked.

"We know that boy didn't have nothing to do with killing his wife."

I stared at her, my mouth hanging open. "Uh. Maw-Maw? We already knew that."

She shook her head. "No, Miss Ghosty Pants, you did not. You thought he didn't have nothing to do with the murder. But then, you thought his brother didn't do it either--least, that's what you thought until you saw the brother give that Howard boy that briefcase. So whatever you think you know, you don't know all of it."

I took a deep breath. "Okay, then. How do we know now that Rick didn't have anything to do with it?"

"Because," she said, "you could see it all over his face, plain as day. He is just a poor little boy all caught up in something he don't even understand." Her voice was sympathetic, and she pursed her lips and shook her head sadly. "Don't even know who his real friends are," she said sadly, almost whispering.

I stopped back by Howard's on our way into Abramsville. To my delight, he was standing in front of the open hood of his SUV, cursing at the engine.

Just for fun, I made a detour through his house and blew out the television and microwave. And then, for good measure, I destroyed his stereo, too. Finally, I shoved as much energy as I could muster into each of the three phones in his house. By the time I left, I was pretty sure he was cut off from everyone except his immediate neighbors.

It was the least he deserved, but as I made my way back to Stephen's car, I realized that the last two days had left me feeling drained.

"What's wrong with you?" Stephen asked as I got into the car.

"What do you mean?"

"Your body. It's all . . ." he waved his hands back and forth in front of his face. "All transparent."

I looked down at myself. Even I could see the edge of the car seat through my legs.

"I just used up a lot making sure Howard couldn't follow us," I said.

"A lot of what?" Stephen asked.

"I don't know," I said irritably. "Energy, I guess. Quit talking. Just drive us to Maw-Maw's."

Once there, Maw-Maw insisted that I have a "little lie-down" in her guest bedroom. I was in no shape to resist, so I took her advice and dropped down onto the bed. I didn't need to lie down to go into my fugue floating state, but it felt good to do so--comforting, familiar.

I closed my eyes and let myself drift.

Chapter Thirteen

I awoke--or at least, came back to myself--to the sound of loud voices coming from the living room.

"Absolutely not," I heard Ashara say loudly

"I am a grown woman, missy, and I will do as I please," Maw-Maw replied, with almost as much force.

"You're an old woman, and you're going to get yourself hurt. Or worse."

"It don't matter what you say, Ashara. I am not going to quit. Callie needs us, and so does that poor Rick McClatchey. We are going to solve this case."

I pulled myself up out of the bed (I realized that I'd actually sunk partway through the mattress in my stupor) and headed toward the living room, ready to wade into the fray.

Ashara spun around to face me as soon as I entered the room.

"And you," she said, pointing her finger at me accusingly, "you're the one who dragged us all into this. It's your fault, you know."

I hung my head. "Yeah," I said. "I know."

Maw-Maw clicked her tongue at me. "Now don't you go taking the blame for something that isn't your fault. Just because Ashara here is scared don't mean that we're gonna up and quit."

"You took my grandmother to a prison," Ashara said, still glaring at me.

"A jail, actually," I said. "There is a difference."

"Not to me, there's not," Ashara said.

"I told you we were going to do it."

"Yeah. At work, where I can't even answer you without everyone thinking I'm totally crazy."

I tried to calm her. "If it's any consolation, I don't think we're going to need to go back. I don't think Rick McClatchey knows anything useful."

Ashara sighed and sank down onto the couch. She

shook her head and spoke more quietly. "It just scares the hell out of me knowing that that murderer is out there loose and knows who we are."

"It scares me, too, Ashara," I said. "Believe me, I don't want either of you getting hurt. Any of you." I looked around the room. "Where's Stephen?"

Ashara stared at me blankly for a moment. "He hasn't been here since he dropped you and Maw-Maw off yesterday afternoon."

Yesterday? I'd been in my fugue state for twenty-four hours. Dammit. Another day lost. I was beginning to think that we needed to move quickly; if we didn't, we might lose track of everyone. And the only way we were going to be able to tell the police what had really happened was if we had some sort of real evidence. Something tangible. Something that would leave them in no doubt that Howard had killed Molly and Jeffrey McClatchey was in on it.

Bags of money passed between two men wasn't going to cut it. It simply wasn't enough.

"Did you find out who the other safe deposit box belonged to?" I asked Ashara.

"Yes," she said. "Someone named Mary Powell."

Powell. I'd heard that name before.

"Did you say Mary Powell?" Maw-Maw said, sitting up straighter in her recliner and staring at Ashara.

"Yes, ma'am," Ashara said, looking confused. "Is that important?"

"Hmm," said Maw-Maw. "Might be."

"Where have I heard that name before?" I asked.

"When I told you about how Jimmy Powell done got into a fight with them Howard boys and disappeared all them years ago."

"Was Mary Powell a relative of his?" I asked.

"All them Powells are related," Maw-Maw answered, waving her hand dismissively in the air.

"Yes, but do you know how Mary Powell was related

to Jimmy?"

"Well, I do believe that both his mother and his sister was named Mary." She nodded her head definitively. "Yep. So there's two Marys right there."

"Did you get anything other than a name?" I asked Ashara.

"Yes. I found out who else was on the signature card: both Rick and Jeffrey McClatchey."

"That's weird," I said.

Ashara nodded. "I also got an address for Mary Powell, but it might be old. The box was paid for at least ten years in advance, but it didn't look like anyone had been in to open it in years. And the McClatchey brothers were added to the signature card only about four years ago."

"You want to drive by the address?" I asked. "It can't hurt to see if there's a name on the mailbox or something."

Ashara sighed. "Okay. Fine."

"I'm coming, too," Maw-Maw announced, heaving herself up out of her chair.

"Of course you are." Ashara sounded resigned.

"So how long ago did Jimmy Powell disappear?" I asked Maw-Maw once we were in the car and headed through town.

"Well, I was just about twenty-one--it wasn't long before I married your grand-daddy, Ashara--so that would have been . . . let me see. . . ." Her eyes flicked back and forth in her head as she figured it out. "Nineteen and forty-seven. All them boys come back from the war and Jimmy Powell was just as pretty as he could be. But he didn't last for more than a year before getting into it with those Howard boys, so it must have been in 'forty-seven that he disappeared."

1947. I wondered if the U.S. government had been making thousand-dollar bills in 1947.

Something was starting to come together, but I still didn't have all the pieces. I couldn't put the ones that I did have together, couldn't see the big picture, but I knew I was getting closer.

*   *   *   *

The house we were looking for was in one of the older neighborhoods in town--much shabbier than the one Maw-Maw lived in. Some of the houses looked like they were barely standing, held together with boards and string and tar-paper. But the address Ashara had led us to was in much better condition. It was tiny, but freshly painted. Azaleas bloomed in a tiny patch of ground in front of the porch, which, unlike the Howard's, did not sag.

"Nice-looking place," I commented to Ashara.

"Mmm," she murmured in agreement.

"Think we should stop in and say hello?" Maw-Maw asked.

Ashara kept driving, right past the house. "No. I don't," she said. "I think we ought to go home and consider what all this might mean. What do you think, Callie?"

I ignored her, too busy staring out the back window to answer her.

"Ashara?" I said nervously.

"Yeah?"

"See that white SUV behind us?"

She looked in the rear-view mirror. "Oh, shit," she said. "Is it Howard?"

Maw-Maw craned her neck around and for once didn't even bother to correct her granddaughter's language.

"I think it might be," I said. "How did he get it running again so fast?"

"Oh," said Maw-Maw. "He's a mechanic."

I looked at her, my eyebrows beetling. "How do you know that?"

"He told me. The same time he told me his name. That day you made us take you out there."

I shook my head in amazement.

"Is he really following us?" Ashara asked. "I mean, maybe he's just out for a drive or something."

"Past the old Powell place. I'm sure," I said.

The SUV slowed behind us as it passed the Powell house, but didn't stop. Instead, he picked up speed and caught up with us.

Ashara drove quickly through the back streets, heading toward Main Street. "Maybe he'll leave us alone once we get downtown," she said hopefully.

The SUV tailed us for a few minutes more, and then abruptly turned off onto another side street.

"Oh, thank God," said Ashara. "He's gone."

"Thank you, Jesus," Maw-Maw added in a fervent tone.

I was just about to add my own prayer to whatever celestial being might take interest in a stranded ghost chick, when suddenly the SUV cut out of a side street right in front of us, slamming to a stop.

Ashara hit the brakes so hard she practically stood up on them and, at the same time, twisted the wheel to avoid hitting the SUV.

She missed it; instead, her front tires bumped over the curb and hit the lawn of the house on the corner.

I've got to hand it to her: that girl is one tough driver. If I'd been behind the wheel, we would have stopped right there, and there's no telling what Howard would have done to us.

Not Ashara, though. As soon as she felt the tires hit grass, she spun the wheel back around and hit the gas as hard as she'd hit the brakes. The back tires squealed and the front tires threw up a shower of grass and dirt, but the car moved, twisting past the SUV and screaming down the residential street.

I saw Howard's face, ugly and red with anger, as we drove past him.

I flipped him the bird.

Okay. So it was crude. But he couldn't see me anyway, so what did it matter?

"Now," I said to Ashara. "Now we go to the police."

"And say what?"

"Report what just happened. That you and your elderly grandmother were out for an evening drive and a crazy man tried to run you off the road."

"What if the police tell him who I am?" she asked.

"He already knows," I reminded her. "And I think it's time we start working on getting him on the police radar. So to speak."

Ashara nodded and took a deep breath. "Okay."

The balding officer who took Ashara's report at the local police station seemed more than a little bored with and skeptical of Ashara's story, but at least he filled out a report, taking down Howard's license plate and a description of the SUV.

"So what happens next?" Ashara asked.

The cop shrugged. "No one was hurt, so there's not much we can do."

"He tried to run me off the road," she said indignantly.

"And we'll send an officer out to speak to him about it. But unless you can come up with a witness--"he paused, glancing at Maw-Maw, "another witness," he corrected himself, "then all we can do is issue him a warning."

Ashara sighed. "Fine. Thanks for all your help."

"Try not to sound so sarcastic," I hissed at her. "You want these guys to take you seriously."

She spun on her heel and marched out of the police station, leaving Maw-Maw to hobble out after her.

"It just makes me so damned mad," she fumed as she got Maw-Maw settled into the car. "I guarantee, if it had been a black man running a white woman off the road, that cop would have been a whole lot more helpful."

I nodded. "You're probably right. But right now we have to accept every little bit of official help we can get."

"That shouldn't mean that I have to swallow my pride and go beg some policeman to help me."

"And you didn't. All you did was file a report. So let's leave it at that for now."

Ashara got into the driver's side and slammed the door.

"Fine," she snarled, looking at me in the rearview mirror. "But as soon as we've got enough on that murdering motherfucker to lock him away forever, we're going straight back into that station and I'm going to shove it in that asshole's face."

"Agreed," I said.

"Ashara," Maw-Maw said reprovingly.

"I'm sorry, Maw-Maw," Ashara said. "It just makes me so angry to get treated like that."

"I know it does, honey. But he'll get his. Don't you worry." She folded her hands over her stomach complacently.

Ashara huffed out a breath and shook her head.

"Let's just go back home," she said.

"Not your place," I reminded her.

"I know, I know." She shook her head. "We need to wrap this up soon--I've got to get back into my house and get some more clothes."

*   *   *   *

"Have you heard from Stephen?" I asked Ashara as we walked back into Maw-Maw's.

She shook her head. "Not since last night. He was still here when I got home from work, but he didn't stay long. I think that visit to Rick McClatchey really shook him up."

"I think it was the first time he'd really thought about what it would mean for Rick to get convicted of this crime," I agreed.

"You think maybe I should call him or something?" Ashara asked.

"It's up to you, but I would if I could. He's trying to help us and now we have new information that he doesn't have."

"I think you ought to call him. He's nice. Especially for a white boy," Maw-Maw opined.

Ashara rolled her eyes and pulled out her pulled out her cell phone and tapped away. *When did they trade numbers?* I wondered.

"Hey, Steve," she said. "Ashara. We've found out some more stuff if you want to hear about it." She waited in silence for a moment. I could hear Stephen talking but couldn't make out the words.

"Yeah, well, the killer tried to run us over tonight," she said. Again, I heard Stephen's voice, this time pitched a little higher.

"No. We're all okay," Ashara said. "Okay," she said after another short silence. "We'll be here." She flipped the phone closed. "He's finishing up something at home, and then he'll be over."

When Ashara answered the door, Stephen stepped in and gave her a quick one-armed hug.

"You doing okay?" he asked.

"Yeah," she said. "You?"

"I'm not the one who just almost got run over by a crazed killer," he said.

"Not yet," I muttered.

"I'm hoping not ever," he said with a sidelong glance at me.

"Hello, Miss Adelaide," he said, leaning over and giving her a peck on the cheek. "I brought you these." He brought his other arm out from behind his back and flourished a bouquet of colorful flowers at her.

"Oh, you sweet boy," Maw-Maw said. And I swear she simpered at him. "Ashara, you go get the vase down from the cabinet over the refrigerator and put these in some water." She held the flowers up to her nose and breathed in deeply. "Mmm," she said. "I always did love me the smell of flowers."

"Kiss up," I mouthed at Stephen behind Maw-Maw's back.

"I heard that, Callie Taylor," said Maw-Maw.

I blinked, surprised.

Ashara came back with the vase and, once the flowers were arranged to Maw-Maw's satisfaction and placed on top of the television where she could see them from her armchair, we all took turns telling Stephen what had happened in his absence.

He let out a low whistle when we'd finished. "So now he knows that we're on to him," he said.

"Or at least that something's up and it involves Ashara," I said.

"That worries me." Stephen's eyebrows beetled and he frowned as he looked at Ashara.

"Not half as much as it worries me," she said.

"I just don't know what we can do about it right now," I said, my voice showing my frustration.

"Well," said Stephen decisively, "I don't think there is anything we can do right now. Have y'all eaten dinner yet?" he asked.

I blinked at the sudden change in topic.

"No, we haven't," said Maw-Maw.

"Well, then," said Stephen, "let's order a pizza and forget about all this for right now. We'll come back to the problem later, after we've all had something to eat and some sleep."

He looked up at me suddenly with a horrified look on his face.

"Oh. Callie. I didn't mean . . ." he stopped, searching for a word.

I laughed. "Trying to apologize to the eating-challenged?"

He blushed.

"Don't worry about it," I said. "I'll just sit here and enjoy the company."

In the end, I enjoyed the smell of the pizza almost as much as the company. Maybe a little more. We were all subdued, worried about what was going to happen next, how we were going to keep everyone safe from Howard until we could pin Molly's murder on him.

None of us came up with any sudden inspirations, though, and when the pizza was gone, Stephen got up to leave.

"I'll walk you to your car," Ashara said.

"No," Stephen and I said in unison.

"You're the only one whose name Howard knows," I reminded her. "If he even happened to drive by and saw you here, then he'd know how to get to your grandmother."

Ashara groaned.

"She's right," Stephen said. He reached up and brushed a curl off her shoulder. "You're safer inside. Stay here. I'll see you tomorrow." He turned and let himself out of the house.

"What was that?" I asked Ashara as she bolted the door behind him.

"What was what?"

"That business with the hair."

"I have no idea what you're talking about. He's just a nice guy."

Maw-Maw and I looked at each other and snickered.

"You two are horrible," Ashara said. "I'm going to bed now. You should too, Maw-Maw."

"No, baby, I'm not tired yet," Maw-Maw said. "I'm going stay up and watch me some TV. I don't got no sweet thoughts of a pretty white boy to rock me to sleep." She grinned evilly at Ashara.

Ashara rolled her eyes again. "Fine," she said. She stalked down the hall and into the third bedroom, slamming the door behind her.

"Just a nice boy," Maw-Maw snorted.

"Sure he is," I said, heading toward the guest room I had claimed as my own.

I heard Maw-Maw cackling behind me as I drifted into that floating fugue state that I was beginning to think of as sleep.

Chapter Fourteen

I awoke--or at least, came to consciousness--sometime in the early hours of the morning. I could hear Maw-Maw snoring loudly in her room and when I poked my head through the door of Ashara's room, I saw that she was curled into a tight ball under the covers, just her dark reddish-brown curls peeking out.

I wandered through the house for a little while trying to decide what our next move should be. Howard's attempt to waylay us the night before had worried me more than I had wanted to let on. I paced back and forth in the living room, trying to put all the pieces together.

So Clifford Howard and Jeffrey McClatchey had somehow conspired to split a bunch of money in a safe deposit box belonging to a Mary Powell, but to which both the McClatchey brothers had access. But only Rick McClatchey had the key. Mary Powell was related to a man who had probably been murdered in the 1940s by men related to Clifford Howard.

I suspected the money in the safe deposit box was somehow connected to the 1940s killing of Jimmy Powell, but I couldn't figure out why Clifford had killed Molly McClatchey. I had no idea where the McClatcheys fit into this at all.

I was still pacing back and forth when Maw-Maw came out of her bedroom wrapped in an old blue terry cloth robe, her hair already tucked into its bun, pieces already escaping to frame her face.

"How's an old woman supposed to sleep with you making all that racket in here?" she asked irritably.

"Racket?" I asked in stunned amazement, looking down at my feet. "I'm floating six inches off the ground. I haven't touched anything. How could I be making a racket?"

"Hmph," the old woman said--which really didn't seem to be much of an answer to me--and stumped off to the kitchen. I heard her start the coffee pot.

"Well," she said, coming back in a little later, steaming coffee cup in hand, "you might as well sit down and talk about what's got you so riled up. I'm awake now."

I suppressed a grin and told her everything I'd been considering.

"Well, now," she said, setting her coffee to one side and leaning her head back against the headrest of her recliner, "let's see." She hummed a little to herself, her eyes closed.

Finally she opened them again. "Well, Mary Powell-- Jimmy's mama--wasn't never the same after he disappeared. She took to spending all her time at home. Before that, she had herself plenty of friends. But my mama said that Jimmy's loss just took all the heart out of Mary." She shook her head, her mouth twisted to the side.

"You said there was a daughter named Mary, too, right?" I asked.

She nodded. "Now she was a scandal."

"Really?" I leaned forward from my seat on the couch.

"Yes, ma'am. She and her mama had opposite reactions to losing Jimmy. Her mama hid out in her house, wouldn't hardly do nothing. But little Mary--she must've been about seventeen at the time--got even worse than she had been, running around with all kinds of boys, drinking, smoking, generally acting up."

"And her mother didn't do anything to stop her?" I asked.

Maw-Maw shook her head. "Not at first. Mind you, she had always been a wild child, and her mother hadn't done nothing about it then. When Jimmy came home, he tried to stop her, but it was tough row to hoe with that one. She never did take to being told what to do."

"But later?"

"Well." And now Maw-Maw was also leaning forward in her chair, her voice dropped low to tell the secret of a sixty-year-old scandal. "Not all too long after Jimmy disappeared,

Miss Mary left town. Her relations here put it out that she was going to go live with some cousins out in Georgia, but we didn't none of us believe it."

"So where do you think she went?" I asked breathlessly, completely drawn into the story.

"She was gone just a little over eight months," Maw-Maw said, leaning back in her chair and nodding complacently, "as those of us was counting figured it. Just about the right amount of time to have herself a little one and then come on home."

"Did she bring the baby back with her?" I asked.

Maw-Maw let out a bark of laughter. "Not then. But it weren't but a few months after that a Powell cousin comes to town and asks if Mrs. Mary--little Mary's mother--could take care of this baby she, the cousin, just ain't got the means for. As if Mary had any more money than anybody else. We all knew it was Miss Mary's baby, but we all pretended we didn't."

I leaned back in my seat, too. "Wow. So whose baby was it? I mean, who was the father?"

Maw-Maw shook her head. "Never did know for sure. Some white man, though, to look at the boy."

Ashara came walking through the doorway into the living room, yawning and grimacing. "What are you two in here talking about? Can't you let a person sleep?" She glared at us briefly, yawned again, and staggered toward the kitchen.

"Neither of you are really morning people, are you?" I asked.

Maw-Maw just shook her head. "Never was able to get that child out of bed. Even when she was a tiny baby, her mama would have to just about lie on top of her to get her to be still enough to go to sleep at night. And once she was asleep, she didn't want nobody waking her up." She smiled.

"What happened to Ashara's parents?"

Ashara walked in with coffee in hand.

"My daddy left when I was just little," she said. "I

hardly remember him."

"He never was no good," Maw-Maw said, her mouth tightening up.

"And Mama died of breast cancer five years ago," Ashara said.

"I'm sorry," I said.

Ashara shook her head. "It's okay. It was hard, but I've still got Maw-Maw." She took her grandmother's hand and squeezed it.

"So what were you talking about?" she asked, sitting down on the other end of the couch and curling her feet under her.

"Miss Adelaide was telling me about the Powell family."

"Yeah?"

So Maw-Maw repeated it. As I listened to it again, the barest hint of an idea began to tickle at the back of my mind.

"What happened to the baby boy?"

"Well, when little Mary finally settled down and married one of the Washington boys, the little boy stayed on with her mother. Guess Miss Mary's new husband didn't have no interest in having her first little one around. Seemed to put the heart back into Mrs. Mary, to some degree, anyway. He growed up to be just almost as pretty as his uncle Jimmy had been."

"Then what?"

"Well," she said, squinting her eyes as she thought. "He went off to Atlanta and married himself a white woman. That was in the seventies, you know, and it was a bit of a scandal, but those two sure did love each other."

"And they had kids?" I asked.

She tilted her head. "Well. I guess I don't rightly know."

I stood up and brushed a kiss toward Maw-Maw's cheek. "Thank you, Miss Adelaide. You've been a big help."

She patted me on my own cheek, her hand sliding

halfway into my face. "I'm glad, Callie, honey."

I turned to Ashara. "You're going to have to call in sick today," I said.

"I can't," she said indignantly. "I'm not sick."

I sighed. "There is a crazy murderer out there who knows where you work and might just be waiting for you there. You can't go to work. You can't even leave this house in your own car. You have to call in sick at least until we get that guy off the streets. But I've got some ideas about that, so if you'll just quit being so damned stubborn, ignore your own work ethic for one day, and come help me, we might be able to fix it so that you never have to call in sick ever again."

Maw-Maw snickered.

Ashara glared first at her, and then at me. "Fine. As soon as the bank opens, I'll let them know."

"Good," I said. "In the meantime, we need to call Stephen. Howard doesn't recognize his car."

"Sure," said Ashara. "Let me get my cell."

Maw-Maw and I glanced at each other.

"You can both just quit it," Ashara said. "Yes, I have his number. He's part of this, too. I knew we might need to get in touch with him."

"Mmm-hmm," Maw-Maw said, clearly humoring her.

Ashara shook her head in irritation and flounced out of the room.

Maw-Maw and I snickered.

A few moments later, Ashara re-entered the living room. "Well," she said, "I woke him up. Hope you're happy."

"Is he coming over here?" I asked.

"Yes."

"Then I'm happy."

She rolled her eyes at me. "He'll be here in about forty-five minutes. I'm going to go take a shower and get dressed."

"Be sure to wear something pretty," Maw-Maw called out after her.

"You are a bad, bad woman," I teased affectionately.

She smiled sweetly. "That's why you like me so much," she said.

Chapter Fifteen

"So we need to find out how the Powells are connected to either the Howards or the McClatcheys," I said after catching Stephen up on the history we'd learned from Maw-Maw.

"Do you have any idea how to do that?" Stephen asked.

"I do," Ashara said. "At least, I know where to start. There's genealogy stuff all over the internet."

"Sounds like a good place to start," I said.

"We can go back to my place," Stephen and Ashara said at the same time.

"Not your place," I said to Ashara. "Clifford Howard knows which street you live on."

"Mine it is, then," Stephen said cheerfully.

Stephen lived in an apartment over one of the old downtown buildings, overlooking the square.

"So what's your theory?" Stephen asked me as the three of us walked in.

"I'm not entirely sure," I said. "But I'm wondering if the white woman that married the Powell boy was a McClatchey. That would explain how Rick McClatchey ended up with the key--maybe it was his aunt or something."

"So how do the Howards fit into this, then?" he asked.

I shook my head. "I don't know. Except that maybe the money in Mary Powell's safe deposit box belonged to the Howards at one point. That would give the Howards a motive for killing Jimmy Powell."

"But where did they get it?" Ashara asked.

"Maybe they had money at some point?" I suggested. "That old house Clifford Howard lives in looks like it might have been a pretty nice farmhouse at some point."

"And if everyone calls it the old Howard place road," Stephen said, "they were probably fairly prominent at some point."

"Well, all that's left now is some creepy psycho killer guy," I said. "And he's not going to go away until we figure out who the money belonged to originally, why the key ended up with Rick and Molly McClatchey, how Clifford Howard found out about it, and why Jeffrey McClatchey didn't just steal it. Why did they have to kill Molly?"

"God," said Ashara, "when you put it that way, it sounds like an awful lot of work."

Stephen bit his lower lip and looked thoughtful. "You know what? I have an idea. You two stay here and do the genealogy research. I'm going to go to the library and look something up."

"Okay," I said. "Want to share?"

He shook his head. "Not yet. Come on in to the bedroom and I'll get the computer started for you."

His room was spare--a bed with a simple quilt, a desk with a computer, and a few bookshelves. I checked the titles on his shelf; I've always thought that the books someone keeps around can tell you a lot about that person. His were almost all labeled "classics"--lots of novels by people like Jane Austen and Thomas Hardy. I'd been an English major in college, but I hadn't read even a third of the books he had on his shelf.

Interesting, I thought. A man who repairs musical instruments and reads nineteenth-century novels. Probably smart, too. Ashara could do a lot worse.

"Okay, then," Stephen said, knocking me out of my reverie. "I'm leaving. Call me on my-cell if you need me. I'll bring lunch with me when I come back."

Ashara waved at him without looking away from the computer screen. She was already absorbed.

Two hours later we were both ready to take a break. Do you have any idea how many Powells, Howards, and McClatcheys are listed on the internet? Yeah. I hadn't realized it, either. Roughly seventy-two bajillion, from what I could tell. We'd eliminated a bunch of them, but hadn't yet come up with the information we wanted.

Ashara stood up and stretched her arms above her head. "Okay," she said. "I'm going to get some water or something."

I nodded, staring at the computer and wishing I could do something more than just look over her shoulder. Sometimes I really hate being incorporeal. Life was easier when I was . . . well, alive.

"Hey!" I said, suddenly hit by an overwhelming desire to connect to my old life. "Can you check my email for me?"

Ashara stared at me. "Callie, honey, I hate to tell you this, but you're dead."

"That doesn't mean that they closed off my email account. No one else even knows the password. Come on. I'm just curious."

So Ashara sat back down, opened a browser, went to my email provider and logged me in. I had 134 new messages.

Most of them were spam.

A few of them were from work colleagues and friends, mostly posted within a day or two of my death, mostly asking if I wanted to get together for lunch or drinks or dinner.

"Doesn't this freak you out at all?" Ashara asked as she opened one of the non-spam messages and let me read it.

I shook my head. "It makes me a little sad, but mostly it reminds me that I really did have a life. A real one, with a job and friends and everything."

Then all the personal emails stopped three days after my death. I guessed that was when the news got around.

Except for one. There was one email at the very bottom of the "new messages" list. It was dated almost two weeks after my death.

It was from my mother.

I pointed to it. "Open that one," I said, my voice hoarse.

"Are you sure?" Ashara asked.

I nodded silently, not trusting my voice.

"My dearest, darling, baby girl," the message began. "I know you'll never get this, but I need to send it."

"Oh, God," I whispered.

Ashara stood up. "I'll leave you alone to read this one."

I won't give you the details. It hurts too much. Suffice to say that it was an expression of my mother's grief and rage and deep loss, emailed out into the void, sent to a daughter she believed would never receive it.

Ghosts can't cry, I discovered as I read it.

For one insane moment, I wanted to ask Ashara to answer it for me. But I knew I couldn't. If I couldn't go to her myself, then I couldn't send my mother an email. She'd think it was a hoax. It would cause her even more hurt than she already felt. I couldn't do that to her.

Ashara came back into the room a few moments later. "Done?" she asked softly.

"Completely," I said. "Remind me never to do that again."

"Agreed," she said. I looked up at her and saw tears in her eyes.

"I kind of wish I could give you a hug right now," she said.

"Yeah. Me, too," I admitted. I took a deep breath--marveling again that I could actually feel as if I were breathing--and said, "Okay, enough weepiness. Let's get back to work."

*   *   *   *

An hour later, we found what we'd been looking for. Unfortunately, it wasn't what I had expected.

The younger Mary Powell had named her son after her brother Jimmy. The elder Mary Powell had brought him up and when he moved to Atlanta, James Powell had married a woman named Gloria Lee. No relation to the McClatcheys.

"Damn," I muttered.

"Double damn," Ashara agreed.

We both jumped when we heard the front door slam.

"It's just me," Stephen called out from the living room. "I brought food in case anyone's hungry."

I followed Ashara into the living room. "I'm not hungry," I said, "but I bet Ashara is. And we've got something to tell you."

"I've got something to tell you, too," Stephen said, excitement in his voice.

"Did you find anything useful?" I asked.

"Maybe." He began pulling burgers and fries out of a paper bag. "You tell me what you found while Ashara and I eat, and then I'll tell you what I found."

My telling didn't take long. I left out the bit about the email from my mother, of course, just sticking to the genealogical search on the Powell family.

"Well," said Stephen, then paused dramatically.

"What?" I demanded.

"I think I figured out where all that money came from."

Ashara stared at him open-mouthed. "Really? Where?"

"Jimmy Powell and the Howard brothers stole it," Stephen announced. "From a bank in Atlanta. They were bank robbers."

Chapter Sixteen

Ashara and I ran over one another answering him. "You're kidding"--"No way"--"Really?"

When we had finally stopped talking, he pulled a file folder out of a backpack lying on the floor next to his plaid couch. In the folder was a sheaf of papers, all photocopies of old newspaper reports about a bank robbery in Atlanta, Georgia.

"Your story about a safe deposit box full of old money made me think about bank robberies," he said. "I mean, where else does anyone get that much cash?"

"But what makes you think it was Jimmy and the Howards?" I asked.

He tried to hand one of the copies to me. I cocked an eyebrow at him and waved a hand through the paper.

"Oh. Right," he said. "I forgot."

"That's okay. Just read it to us."

"It's short," he said. Stephen cleared his throat and began to read aloud.

"Dateline. Atlanta, Georgia, July 25, 1947. Yesterday morning, three armed gunmen robbed Atlanta's Fourth Federal Bank."

"Fourth Federal?" interrupted Ashara. "Who banks at Fourth Federal? Who names a bank Fourth Federal?"

"Do you want to hear the rest of the article or not?" Stephen said.

"Okay, okay. I'll shut up. But still. Fourth Federal." She shook her head.

Stephen smiled and continued reading.

"The gunmen are believed to have gotten away with over $50,000 in cash."

Ashara let out a low whistle. I nodded. I didn't think that there had been quite so much in the safe deposit box, but then, some of it might have been spent. And how would I know what fifty grand in cash looked like, anyway? I was a ghost who used to design pamphlets for phone companies.

"Witness say that the three men were wearing masks. However, at least one witness claims that two of the men were white, but that the third man was a Negro." He paused over the word, shaking his head briefly before continuing.

"At this time, police are claiming no leads in the case. Anyone with any further information about the case is urged to come forward."

He looked up. "That's about it."

"So what makes you so sure these bank robbers are Jimmy Powell and the Howard brothers?" I asked.

Stephen shook his head. "I'm not, entirely. But it makes sense."

"Why Atlanta?" Ashara asked. "Birmingham's closer."

"That may be exactly why they chose Atlanta," Stephen said. "It's far enough away that no one is likely to recognize them."

"And Fourth Federal couldn't have been one of your bigger banks," I said, "so they might have felt safer going after it."

"And it explains why Jimmy Powell got into it with the Howards," Ashara said. "That much money in 1947? It'd be enough to kill for."

Stephen and I nodded.

"But how can we be sure the money came from that particular bank robbery?" I asked.

"There'll be records," Ashara said confidently. "Serial numbers, that sort of stuff. Even Bank South has records going back to the 30s and 40s."

"But does Fourth Federal even still exist?" I asked.

"Actually, it does," Stephen said. "I checked that out, too."

Ashara smiled at him admiringly. I pretended not to notice.

"Okay, then," I said. "I guess the next thing is to get at least one of those bills."

"Were there any five-hundred-dollar bills?" Ashara asked.

"I don't remember seeing any," I said. "Why?"

"Because either a five hundred or a thousand-dollar bill would be best," Ashara said. "Those are the least common, the easiest to trace."

"Okay. So we need a big bill," I said.

"You know," said Ashara thoughtfully, "those high-denomination bills haven't been in circulation for ages. They stopped printing them in the thirties, I think. They'd be worth a lot more than their face value now."

We all stared at each other for a long moment.

"So," Stephen finally said. "How do we go about stealing a thousand-dollar bill from one of these guys?"

"I'll have to go in and figure out where they're hiding the money," I said. "But then y'all are going to have to go in to actually get the bill. On accounta I'm dead and all. Makes it hard to carry things."

Stephen gave me a sidelong glance.

"Sorry," I said. "I get sarcastic when I get nervous."

"I'm beginning to notice that."

I took a deep non-breath. "Okay, then. I'll start at Jeffrey McClatchey's--he seems less dangerous. He hasn't actually cut anyone into tiny pieces."

"That we know of," Ashara said.

"Great," I said. "Thanks for the reminder."

She shrugged. "We need to remember to keep our guard up. Just because he didn't kill Molly doesn't mean he isn't capable of killing one of us."

Stephen nodded. "She's right."

"I still say he's the lesser of the two evil dudes," I said.

"Oh, hell yeah," said Ashara. "Definitely hit his place first."

"Okay. I'll be back in a bit to tell you what I find."

"We'll be waiting," Stephen said.

*   *   *   *

It took me a while to find Jeffrey McClatchey's house again--I'd only been there once, after all. But I did finally find it. Eventually. All those subdivisions looked the same to me.

I poked my head in through the door, waiting to see if an alarm went off. None did, so I slipped into the house. In retrospect, it probably would have made more sense to go in through a wall or a window--someplace less likely to have an alarm attached to it. I'm still getting used to this being a ghost business.

The house was empty. I started in the bedroom, looking for the bag of cash he'd stuffed under his car seat.

It wasn't in the closet. Or under the bed. Or under the sink in the bathroom, or under the couch in the living room, or in the vegetable crisper in the refrigerator. It wasn't in any of the places that I would have tried to hide it if I'd had a bag full of money.

I heaved a sigh and stood in the middle of the living room. Where else might a thirty-something man hide a briefcase full of extraordinarily valuable bills?

A single thirty-something man. What did I know about single thirty-something men?

Well, I used to date some of them. Not that my dating experience was going to be of any help here. I could pretty much claim with impunity and complete honesty that every single thirty-something man that I had personally dated had had something terribly wrong with him. If he hadn't, he would have been married by then. At least, that was the conclusion I'd come to when I was still alive.

Then again, there was clearly something wrong with this guy, too. He'd been involved in having his sister-in-law chopped into little bitty bits.

And then it hit me. The biggest stereotype in the book. Single men don't cook. I knew it wasn't true; I'd gone out with some men who had cooked extraordinarily well. But it was worth a try.

The oven was empty. On second thought, the oven

might not be anyone's first choice, particularly someone who didn't want to cook the big pile of money he'd just gotten.

I spent another hour looking in every spot I could think of. And some that just caught my attention as I passed by. I don't know until then that I could search a house quite so thoroughly.

"Dammit," I said aloud. "Where did you put it?"

He'd only had it for a little while. He hadn't had all that long to stash it away.

Maybe he has it with him, I thought. If I had a briefcase full of cash, I might not want to let it out of my sight. For all I knew, it might still be shoved under the passenger seat of his car.

I let out several loud curses--the sort that Maw-Maw might have washed my mouth out with soap for, if I'd had a real mouth to wash out.

I was going to have to go to Clifford Howard's house and see if I could find the money there.

And I couldn't leave town without Maw-Maw.

More curses. I was glad Maw-Maw wasn't here.

With a huge sigh, I went back to Stephen's.

I walked in on them kissing. Stephen and Ashara. On the couch. Total make-out session. Oops. I guess that's what I get for walking in through locked doors. *Well,* I thought, *that progressed faster than I thought it would.* I ducked back out of the room and made a big show of calling out as I re-entered through the door, swinging my leg in first to give them a chance to disengage. Untangle themselves. Whatever.

It didn't give Stephen time to wipe the red lipstick smears off his mouth, but I declined to mention that. They made a cute couple. No need to discourage them, I decided.

"Any luck?" Ashara asked. She seemed a lot more composed than Stephen, who was blushing a little.

"Nope," I said, ignoring Stephen's discomfort. "If the money's in Jeffrey McClatchey's house, I sure can't find it. And I can't get out to Howard's without Maw-Maw with me."

"Okay, then," said Stephen, finally composing himself enough to speak. "Let's go."

Maw-Maw, of course, was thrilled to be back in on the action.

"Just let me get my purse and my cane, honey," she said to me, turning off the television with the remote control and heaving herself up out of her chair.

We all piled into Stephen's car. Stephen and I agreed that we needed to keep Ashara's car completely away from anything having to do with Howard, but Ashara insisted on going with us.

"I am not about to let you go dragging my grandmother off without me," she said.

"And you want to be in on it if we find the cash," I said.

"That, too," she agreed.

We followed the same plan as before--they parked off the side of the highway in a spot where they could see the old Howard place road but out of the immediate line of sight of anyone coming down the road and turning onto the highway. They were supposed to wait for me there. That was the plan.

It was a good plan.

It would have worked, too. If only they had stuck to it.

*   *   *   *

Howard, of course, was home when I got to his place. *So even if I find the cash,* I thought, *it's going to be harder for Ashara and Stephen to get in to grab some of it.* This was turning out to be a much more frustrating task than I had anticipated.

But he couldn't see me, so I had free reign to search the place.

He was lying on the couch watching television. Not the old television. I'd apparently destroyed that one. But he'd apparently spent some of his new pile of cash on a new one.

And he wasn't watching *Law and Order,* the show that Maw-Maw had been watching when we'd picked her up that afternoon, but one of those trashy small-claims courtroom reality shows. You know, the kind where some guy's pissed off because his roommate moved out without paying the last month's rent, so he pawned the roommate's television to make up for it? Yeah. That kind of show.

Maw-Maw has much better taste in television, I thought. No big surprise there.

The money wasn't under the couch. It wasn't in the toilet tank (and if you think it's not weird to stick your head inside a toilet tank--even if you're a ghost and can't get wet-- then you're wrong. It's totally weird). It wasn't in any of the places that it hadn't been in McClatchey's house.

I had been in the house for almost an hour searching when I finally realized that the most likely place for the money was that rolltop desk. The one I hadn't been able to see in before.

I cursed again.

I know, I know. How can I possibly see inside a toilet tank and not inside the desk? I have no idea. I just can't. Maybe it's an evil desk and I'm a good spirit and therefore can't see in it. Of course, that would mean that the toilet was a good toilet. So that's probably not it. The best theory I've got is that the wood of that desk is so dark and heavy that it doesn't let any light in at all. And apparently, I've got to have at least some light to see by.

Still, I tried. I poked my head inside it once again, just in case.

Nothing but blackness.

So there I was, standing in the middle of the living room, glaring at the rolltop desk, listening to Judge Judy--or someone like her--handing out criticism and judgments, when I heard a knock at the door.

It was Stephen. I looked out the window and saw him standing there, plain as day. Howard looked up suspiciously at the closed door, but made no move to get up off the couch and open it.

"What the hell?" I muttered. Stephen saw me through the window and waggled his eyebrows at me. I waved my hands at him wildly in what I was pretty sure was a "No! Howard's here! Go away!" kind of motion. As a matter of fact, I actually started yelling those exact words, so I'm certain he got the message.

He knocked on the door again, this time harder.

With a grumble, Howard sat up, scratching his chest through his wife-beater t-shirt. He yawned, stood up, and opened the door, staring blankly at Stephen through the screen door.

"Yeah?" he said.

"Hi," said Stephen, in his brightest I'm-not-a-threat kind of voice. "Listen, man, I got a flat down the road--on the highway, actually--and I was wondering if you had a jack I could borrow. I can't figure out where mine's got to."

"Stephen," I said quickly. "I think the money's in this rolltop desk here, but I can't see into it."

Stephen didn't acknowledge my words with even a flicker of an eye. He just kept looking at Howard expectantly.

Howard stared back at him, still suspicious. "The highway? That's almost three miles down the road. Why'd you walk all the way up here?"

"You're the first one who's answered the door." Stephen shook his head and gestured back behind him at the dirt road. "Maybe they're at work or something. Or not willing to open the door to a stranger. I'm just glad someone was home finally."

Howard nodded after another slow moment. "Yeah. Okay. Sure, man. I got a jack in my truck." He flipped the latch on the screen door and went out onto the porch.

They walked over to the SUV and I trailed along behind them. "We can come back later and get the cash," I said to Stephen. "We'll just have to make sure he's not home when we do."

It was a good plan. I know it was.

Howard opened the back door of the SUV and started rummaging.

"Dude," said Stephen. "Can I grab a drink of water? I've been walking a while now."

"Sure," said Howard distractedly, still searching for the jack. "Kitchen's in the back. Help yourself."

What? I thought. *He calls Ashara names for asking directions but sends Stephen into his house without going with him? What a pig.*

Stephen stepped into the house casually, and then walked over to the roll top desk. I followed him.

"What are you doing?" I asked. "We need to wait until he's gone. You can't do this now." My voice went up several notches with every sentence.

Stephen still didn't answer. He just slid the top of the desk open.

"I knew it," I said. I'd been right. There it was. The briefcase, and lucky for us, it wasn't even locked--it popped open at a touch. Stephen reached in and grabbed a five-hundred dollar bill, shoved it into his pocket, then closed the case rolled the desktop back down.

I couldn't believe it had been that easy.

"I found it." Howard's voice came from the front porch. He was heading into the house.

"You don't have water, Stephen!" I was practically screeching at this point.

"Great," Stephen said, stepping away from the desk and into the middle of the room.

"You find the kitchen okay?" Howard asked as he walked in. He looked suspicious again, but he handed the jack to Stephen.

"Sure did. Thanks, man. And thanks for the jack. I'll get it back to you in a few minutes." Stephen sounded perfectly calm and controlled.

I had to admit that I was impressed. To myself. Not out loud to Stephen.

"Let me give you a ride down to your car," Howard said, watching Stephen carefully.

This did get just the tiniest flicker of a nervous response from Stephen. His eyes twitched toward me and widened just the slightest bit.

"No, thanks," he said. "I'll just walk back. No big deal."

But Howard had caught the same response I had. "I insist," he said. His voice was still friendly enough, but his eyes had gone hard and cold. He dropped a beefy hand onto Stephen's shoulder and squeezed. "I insist."

Stephen might have had the stones to come waltzing into the guy's house and steal a five-hundred dollar bill, but he was still a slight man. Taller than Ashara, but not a big guy. Howard outweighed him by at least fifty pounds of muscle.

"Sure," Stephen said, wincing only slightly. "No problem."

"Good." Howard moved toward the SUV.

"Oh, God," I said. "I'll see what I can do."

I had figured out how to move quickly, but I hadn't until that afternoon figured out just how swift I could be.

I'm pretty fast for a dead chick, as it turned out.

I made it back to the car in ten seconds flat. Too bad they don't have a "Dead Chick Flying" event in the Olympics. I'd win hands down.

Ashara was sitting in the driver's seat, fiddling with the radio. Maw-Maw was snoozing in the passenger seat, snoring gently.

I came flying in through the back windshield and landed on the back seat, talking almost as quickly as I had moved to get there.

"Get out!" I yelled. "You've got to get out. Howard's on his way here with Stephen. Hide!"

Maw-Maw jerked awake. I've got to hand it to her--she is one quick old woman. "Come help me out of this seat, Ashara. Now."

Ashara was still trying to take it all in.

"Now!" Maw-Maw and I yelled at the same time.

Ashara threw the door open and ran around to the other side of the car. Maw-Maw already had the door open and was scooting her legs out onto the dirt beside the car.

Ashara helped her out, and they moved into the underbrush.

"Maw-Maw," said Ashara, "you can't hide in all this."

"Don't you back-talk me, young lady. You help me sit down under this here bush."

"Oh, my God," Ashara muttered. "I can't believe we're doing this."

"Hurry," I said. "Hurry!"

Ashara got Maw-Maw settled out of sight. She started to sit down beside her.

"Wait!" I said. "The tire! You've got to flatten one of the tires. Oh, God. Move it!"

Ashara stared at me blankly for just a second, and then jumped up.

"What has that idiot boy done?" she demanded.

"The glove box," I said. "Maybe there will be something in the glove box."

There was. A screwdriver.

"Great," I said. "Jam it into one of the tires."

It took her two tries, but Ashara did it. The air came whooshing out of the tire. I could see the car sinking as the tire flattened.

"Great. Now shut the doors and hide."

Ashara got into her hiding place next to Maw-Maw mere seconds before Howard drove up in his SUV, Stephen in the passenger seat beside him. I could see Stephen scanning the car. A look of relief and then slight horror crossed his face as he saw the flattened driver's side tire.

But Clifford Howard's face went from suspicious to relaxed, so I decided it had been worth it.

I could see Stephen surreptitiously searching for Maw-

Maw and Ashara as he got out of the car.

"Don't worry," I said, moving up behind him. "They're hidden." He jumped a little at the sound of my voice, but didn't turn around to look at me.

"I'll help you change this," Howard said. He was in full friendly good-ole-boy mode now.

"I'd sure appreciate that," Stephen said, matching his tone. "Why don't you get the jack set while I dig out the spare?"

Howard nodded and settled down to crawl under the car. Stephen popped open the trunk. There, plain as day was a jack.

"Good thing he didn't look in here," I said. Stephen just nodded and pulled out the tire iron and a spare.

"Jack's ready," Howard said.

They changed the tire in mere minutes. I was impressed. I'd had to change a tire myself once when I was alive. It was a pain in the ass. It had taken me almost half an hour.

Stephen hurried to toss the ruined tire into the trunk over his own jack before Howard could see inside.

"Thanks, dude," he said, holding out his now-greasy hand to shake Howard's.

"No problem," Howard said. "You know, it looks like somebody did that tire on purpose."

Stephen made a face. "Ex-girlfriend. She's pissed off 'cause I'm seeing someone else."

"Bitch," Howard said.

"Mmm," Stephen agreed, "you're not kidding."

"Okay, then," said Howard. "Looks like you're all set." He made no move to get into his SUV.

Stephen hesitated, and then decided to roll with it. "Thanks again, man," he said, climbing into the driver's side and turning over the engine. "See you around."

I slid through the passenger door and onto the seat next to him.

Stephen waved as we pulled onto the highway and headed toward town.

"We're going to have to go back for Ashara and Maw-Maw, you know."

"I know. But we need to wait until Howard leaves. I think he's still a little suspicious."

"I'll meet you at the city limits sign," I said as we started to pass it.

Stephen had just enough time to say "What?" before I felt that rubber-band feeling in my gut. Then *pop!* There I was, standing in the middle of a tree trunk next to Maw-Maw.

"Ugh," I said, stepping out of the tree. "That's creepy."

"You think it's creepy for you," Ashara said, "you should have seen how you looked with just your face and boobs sticking out of the tree."

I shuddered. "Don't tell me these things. Howard gone?" I asked.

"Yep," said Maw-Maw. "Got in his car and drove back down the road. We was just sitting here waiting on y'all."

"Okay," I said. "Let me check to make sure Howard went home, then I'll go get Stephen to come back."

Howard was back on his couch.

Stephen was waiting at the city limits sign, a confused look on his face.

And Maw-Maw and Ashara were glad to get out of the scratchy underbrush and back into Stephen's car.

*   *   *   *

"But it still doesn't explain the connection to the McClatcheys," I said. We were back at Maw-Maw's house; all sitting around the living room staring at the bill Stephen had pulled out of his pocket and put on the coffee table. "Even if we can prove it came from the bank robbery in the forties, it doesn't tell us why Howard killed Molly."

We all stared at the bill some more.

"And anyway," I said, "it's not like the police can use it to prove anything. We got it illegally. We didn't have a search warrant or anything."

"That's not true, missy," Maw-Maw said. "Ain't you never watched *Law and Order*? Or *CSI*?"

"Yes," I said defensively. "That's how I know you need a warrant to get evidence."

Maw-Maw shook her head sadly. "Honey, you just ain't paid enough attention. Only the police need a warrant. Private citizen can go on in and take anything. It's stealing, but it can be used as evidence in a court of law."

"Really?"

"Really."

"Well," I said. "Clearly I haven't watched enough of those shows."

"Clearly," said Maw-Maw, leaning back and putting her hands over her stomach.

"That still doesn't help us figure out how to match this bill up with the McClatcheys, other than them having access to the safe deposit box," Ashara said glumly.

"I have an idea," Stephen said. "Why don't I just go back over to Birmingham and ask Rick? He'll probably know what his connection to those two families is."

Ashara and I stood staring at him, our mouths hanging open. Then we looked at each other.

"Do you feel stupid?" I asked her.

"Totally. You?"

"Oh. Beyond words."

We turned back to Stephen. "Yes, please," I said. "Go and ask the one person who might actually know." I shook my head.

"I say that we claim we're still getting used to this detective business," Ashara said to me in a staged aside.

"And hey, I'm still getting over the shock of my untimely death," I said.

Maw-Maw just laughed. "That's one smart white boy you got, Ashara."

Ashara ignored her.

Stephen laughed at us all. "I won't be able to go until tomorrow," he said to Ashara. "I've got to go get a new tire first." He gave her a mock-severe look, and then smiled. "But I'll give you a call as soon as I've finished talking to Rick."

We spent a few more minutes discussing the next day's agenda. I had a hard time deciding whether to stay with Ashara and Maw-Maw or go with Stephen. If I'd wanted to go, we would have had to take Maw-Maw. And if Maw-Maw had gone, Ashara would have, too. Stephen suggested that perhaps one visit from Maw-Maw was plenty for Rick McClatchey. We decided to let Stephen fly solo.

We would have done better to go with him.

Ashara walked Stephen to the door. Then they stepped outside to say goodnight. Maw-Maw and I looked at each other meaningfully. Maw-Maw cackled. And I have to admit that I joined in a little. They were just so cute, acting like teenagers who didn't want anyone to know they were an item.

And hey. I was glad that at least someone was getting some action.

Chapter Seventeen

When I drifted back to myself the next morning, Ashara was already up and dressed. She and Maw-Maw were drinking coffee in the living room and having a serious discussion about something.

"What's up?" I asked as I entered the room.

"Little Miss here thinks she's going to go into work today," Maw-Maw said.

"I don't just think it," Ashara said, more calmly than I would have expected. "It's the truth."

"You can't," I said. "Howard's out to get you."

"I can't keep calling in sick, either," she said. "I have a mortgage to pay. And some credit card bills. And a serious need to buy food sometimes."

"You can just move right back in here with me, Ashara Jones," Maw-Maw said.

"No, Maw-Maw, I can't."

"So what do you propose to do to keep Howard away from you?"

"He didn't seem too anxious to find me yesterday," Ashara said. "You said he was on his ass on the couch watching *Court TV*."

"Well. Yeah," I said. "But that doesn't mean that he didn't go by the bank at some point. He knows where you work, Ashara. And by now he probably knows where you live, too. It's not like I've been following him around twenty-four/seven, shorting out computers all over town. He's certainly looked it up by now."

"But he's not going to do anything while I'm actually in the bank." Ashara shook her head. "I have to go to work. That's it. No more discussion." She drained her cup and went to the kitchen. I could hear her rinsing it out in the sink.

"Isn't Stephen supposed to call you once he's finished talking to Rick McClatchey this morning?" I asked her.

"Yes."

"So how can you possibly take that call if you're at work?"

"I'll keep my cell on vibrate. I am allowed to take breaks, you know."

I sighed. "At least wait for Stephen to get back to town so he can follow you home after work?"

Ashara nodded. "I can do that."

"And promise not to leave the bank at all today until then?"

"Yes."

"Okay, then," I said. "I'm going to ride to work with you to make sure you get there safely."

"Yeah?" said Ashara. "And what are you going to do if something happens?"

"Rush back here and have Miss Adelaide call 911."

"Oh. That's actually not a bad plan," Ashara said. "Okay, then. Let's go."

We were both quiet on the way to the bank until Ashara said, "I have another reason for going in today."

"What's that?" I asked.

"I wrote down the serial number of that bill you and Stephen got yesterday. I'm going to make some calls during my lunch hour and see if I can find out whether or not it really was the one stolen from that bank in Atlanta."

"Really? You can do that?"

She shrugged. "I can try."

We made it to the bank without incident.

Maw-Maw and I spent the rest of the day watching *Law and Order* re-runs on television. At one point, she waved her hand at the screen. "See? What did I tell you? Private citizens don't need no warrant."

"No, ma'am," I said. "They clearly don't."

It was strangely relaxing, spending the day with Maw-Maw. She didn't make any demands, didn't ask any awkward questions.

It was a peaceful day.

If I'd known how long it was going to be before I had another day that peaceful, I would have savored it a bit more.

I got Maw-Maw to call Ashara at noon.

"Anything yet?" Maw-Maw asked. I leaned my head in close to hers in order to listen in on the conversation.

"Not yet," she said. "I'll call you as soon as I hear from him."

She finally called us at three. "Stephen's back in town," she said. "He's meeting me here and then we'll come over there. I don't know what he found out--he said he wants to wait until we're all together so he only has to tell it once."

"Oh, my God," I said into the receiver Maw-Maw was holding. "I can't believe you didn't make him tell you. That's crazy-making."

Ashara laughed. "I tried, but he wasn't having none of it. So we'll see you in a couple of hours."

Stephen followed Ashara home from work that afternoon. We think now that that was probably when Howard started putting everything together--he either followed them then or later that day and figured out that the guy he'd helped change a tire was connected to the pretty black girl he'd been following. Or rather, we think he started putting together *almost* everything, anyway. He couldn't have known about the whole dead chick watching him kill Molly, working on getting his ass thrown in jail, searching his house, and such business.

But of course, we had no idea Howard was on to us, so we just went on with our plans.

Maw-Maw and I had spent much of the afternoon speculating on what Stephen had found out from Rick. But nothing we came up with--none of it very plausible, to be honest--even came close to what he announced after we'd all gotten settled in Maw-Maw's living room.

"Are y'all ready for this?" he asked, pausing dramatically.

"Tell!" Ashara demanded.

"Rick McClatchey's wife, Molly McClatchey. . . ." he

paused again, looking around the room at each of us.

"Enough already. Quit with the drama and just tell us," I said.

Stephen grinned. "Her maiden name? Mary Ellen Powell."

We all gasped.

"As in James Powell?" I asked.

"As in," Stephen said, nodding. "Daughter of James Powell and Gloria Lee Powell of Alabama."

"Damn," Ashara said, on a long exhale.

"Ashara," Maw-Maw warned.

"I'm just saying what we're all thinking, Maw-Maw," Ashara said.

"She's right, Miss Adelaide," I said. "This is the connection we've been looking for."

"Still doesn't tell us how Clifford Howard got involved," Maw-Maw said.

"You know what? I've actually got some ideas on that," I said. "But I'll need some help from Ashara and Stephen on the research end. I think we can probably start with the internet, but it might take a little more than that. Maybe a trip to Atlanta?"

Ashara and Stephen nodded. Maw-Maw rubbed her hands together with glee. "And if you're going to Atlanta," she said to me, "you can't go without me."

"I wouldn't dream of it, Miss Adelaide," I said, smiling.

*   *   *   *

We stopped by Ashara's place for her to pick up some new clothes; she said if she was going to keep working, she needed more than the three outfits she kept at Maw-Maw's. Stephen tried to argue with her--he said that he wore pretty much the same three outfits to work every week--but I had to agree with Ashara. Men, we explained, could get away with that more than women could. And even these extraordinary circumstances couldn't change that fact.

So we stopped in front of her house and they went inside, Stephen leading the way after she'd unlocked the door--just to check things out, he said.

I stayed outside, drifting around the perimeter of the house and keeping watch. Only one car drove by the whole time, and it wasn't Howard's SUV.

After a while, though, I got bored. They seemed to be taking an awfully long time to just "grab a few clothes." So I stuck my head in through the door and called out.

"What are you two doing? Hurry it up!"

I heard a strange scuffle in one of the bedrooms. "Nothing," Ashara called out.

My eyes narrowed. If they had chosen this time for a make-out session, I might have to kill them. See how they liked being the dead ones, for a change.

I slid into the house and followed Ashara's voice. They were indeed sitting on a bed, but they had a laptop in front of them.

"What the hell are you doing?" I demanded. "We need to get out of here before Howard shows up and kills you both." I shook my head in disgust. "What was so important that you had to deal with it here?"

I moved around behind them so that I could see the screen. Ashara closed the computer.

"What?" I asked.

"Nothing," Ashara said again. Her voice cracked.

"Liar," I said. "You two are acting like I caught you looking at porn or something. What gives?"

Stephen sighed. "You might as well show her," he said.

"You think so?"

He nodded. "Yeah."

She flipped up the screen.

It was an article from the *Dallas Morning News*.

About my murder.

"You two looked me up?" I asked incredulously.

"Well," said Ashara, "yeah. We were . . . you know. Curious."

"Great," I said. "You risk your lives to look me up on the internet." I shook my head. "Come on. Get your clothes and let's get out of here. You can look me up again over at Stephen's if you want to."

Back in the car, though, I couldn't contain my own curiosity. "So what did the article say about me?" I asked.

They seemed reluctant to answer.

"I was there, you know," I said. "You're not going to tell me anything I don't already know."

Ashara took a deep breath. "It said you were found murdered and . . ."

"And raped," I said in my most matter-of-fact voice. "I assumed they'd figure out that part."

"Does that not bother you?" Ashara asked in a small voice.

"It bothers the hell out of me," I said. "Did you find out anything about the guy who did it?"

Stephen shook his head. "It said you were his second victim. There have been two others since then."

I stared at them for a long, silent moment.

"You mean that son of a bitch is still out there raping and killing women?" I asked, my voice harsh and dry sounding. It wasn't really a question. I never felt so powerless in my life. Fine. Afterlife.

"Yeah." Ashara's voice was a soft whisper.

"And I'm stuck in fucking Alabama trying to get some schmuck who killed one woman put away." I slammed my hand into the back seat of the car--rather ineffectively, since my hand slid through the leather and into the seat, halfway up to my elbow.

"You're doing good here," Stephen said. I'm sure he was trying to make me feel better.

"And who the hell is out there doing good for all those women in Dallas?" If I'd been alive, tears would have welled up in my eyes. As it was, my mouth just tightened as I stared out the window.

"You don't know," Ashara said. "Maybe some other ghost is out there trying to solve your murder."

"Great," I muttered. "Maybe Molly McClatchey and I traded places."

"You never know," Stephen said. "Stranger things have happened." He paused for a minute. "Actually, I take that back. I'm not sure stranger things have happened. But it's not totally out of the question, given your own presence here."

We pulled up into the parking lot of Stephen's apartment building.

I sighed. "Well, in the end, I am here, and nothing seems likely to change that anytime soon. So we might as well keep working on this murder. Maybe we can go figure my murder out when we're done with this one."

Neither Stephen nor Ashara answered me. I either didn't sound very convincing, or they didn't know what to say to the angry dead chick in the back seat.

                    *   *   *   *

"So what are we looking for?" Stephen asked as he dragged an extra chair over to the computer so that both he and Ashara could sit. I hovered behind them, leaning forward slightly so I could see.

"I want to know who James Powell's father was. The James who was named after Jimmy Powell the bank robber."

"You think we can find that information?" Ashara asked.

"I don't know if we can find it online, but we might be able to find it in Atlanta. Still, I think checking the internet is worth a try."

"Do you think the father's name would even be recorded?" Stephen asked.

"I don't know," I said. "But I know that if I were the one to get pregnant, I'd want to make sure the deadbeat dad who helped get me there was in the records somewhere."

"I don't know," Ashara said. "The forties were a different time."

"But people don't change all that much," I said.

Stephen was already typing search terms into Google. "This may take a while," he said.

"That's okay," I said. "I've got nowhere else to be."

"Me, either," Stephen said. "Work's been slow lately, what with the boss in jail and possibly headed to prison and all."

"But I do have to go to work tomorrow," Ashara said.

"If you get tired, you can just crash here," Stephen said.

I'll just bet she can, I thought. But I kept the thought to myself.

As Stephen narrowed the search and began scanning through websites, I turned to Ashara. "So did you find out anything about the bill?" I asked.

She nodded. "I sure did. It definitely came from the Atlanta robbery. And I also found out that the bills were discontinued in the thirties. So those bills were already old when Jimmy Powell and the Howard brothers stole them."

"That seems kind of odd," I said. "If they were discontinued almost twenty years before the robbery, wouldn't they have been kind of rare?"

Ashara shrugged. "Maybe not. Remember, this wasn't all that long after the Depression. People who had lost money in the market crash were probably unwilling to trust banks for a long time. There were some people who had probably stashed away their cash--under mattresses, in iceboxes, in jars buried in the ground."

"But probably not in the oven," I muttered, thinking about my search of Jeffrey McClatchey's house.

"What?" Ashara asked, her brow wrinkling in confusion.

"Nothing," I said. "I guess you had to be there."

She shook her head again and turned back to the

computer and Stephen.

"Find anything?" she asked.

"Well," he said, "I've been searching the genealogy sites and have found seven James Powells born in Georgia within the right time frame. I'm giving it a three-year window, just in case Miss Adelaide was wrong about the exact year this all happened."

"But no clue about which one is our James Powell?"

He shook his head. "No. If I'd thought to ask, Rick might have been able to tell me." He shrugged. "Then again, maybe not, he was pretty upset about what Miss Adelaide said to him about his brother."

"What did she say?" Ashara asked.

"I'd forgotten you weren't there," I said. We repeated to her what Maw-Maw had told Rick McClatchey about his brother.

Ashara closed her eyes and shook her head. "She's right, of course, but sometimes that woman don't have a lick of diplomacy."

"You sounded exactly like her just then," Stephen said, grinning.

"Yeah, I know. I suffer from the same problem," Ashara said.

Stephen printed out a list of James Powells and their respective birth dates and places. "Okay," he said. "It looks like it's going to be a trip to Atlanta tomorrow to see if we can find these birth records."

"Wait a minute," said Ashara. "Try just looking up 'Georgia birth records'."

We waited for a minute while Stephen scrolled through a page.

"Cool!" he said. "We could order them online." He started typing information into the computer, then stopped.

"Wait," he said. "Okay. Listen to this. Under the 'Birth Certificates' heading, it says this: 'Georgia law and Department Regulation limits access to these documents to the person named and parents shown on the birth records, and the authorized legal guardian or agent, grandparent, adult child, or spouse.' Does that mean we're not allowed to see them?"

Ashara and I both leaned in closer to read the text.

"I think so," I said. "That's really weird. Especially if you're looking for a birth certificate that's at least sixty years old."

Stephen leaned his elbow onto the desk and rested his chin in his hand. He started tapping his chin with his forefinger.

"If we can't find the records there," he began, "then maybe . . ."

". . . They're at Molly McClatchey's," I finished for him.

Ashara nodded. "Makes sense. It is her grandmother we're talking about, after all."

"Unless the family tried to hide from her father that he was really the younger Mary's son," I said.

Stephen shrugged. "We won't know until we try," he said.

"So, shall we go?" I asked.

"Now?" Ashara's eyes grew round.

"I can't think of a better time," I said. "It's dark, so no one will see us. No one is watching the place. It's the perfect time."

"Or it's just possible that you're wrong," Ashara said. "It's dark, so anyone who does see us is going to know we're up to no good."

"Oh, come on," I said. "Anyone who sees us going into Rick McClatchey's house at any time is going to wonder what we're up to. This is the biggest news story to hit this town in years. If we get caught, we're going to have a lot of explaining to do." I paused for a moment. "Or at least, you are. They won't know I'm there."

"Then why don't you just go look?" Ashara said.

"Because I can't move things very easily. And

paperwork like that is going to be filed away. I need someone with a real body to come with me."

"Now, girls, don't fight," Stephen said.

Ashara and I both whirled on him. "Don't call us girls," we said in unison. Then we looked at each other and burst into laughter.

"So we're breaking into Rick McClatchey's house tonight?" I asked.

"Absolutely," said Ashara.

"Women," said Stephen, shaking his head. "I'll never really understand them, will I?"

"Nope," Ashara and I replied in unison.

Chapter Eighteen

Stephen pulled in and parked one street behind McClatchey's house. The sun had set and darkness settled in over the town. "We'll be able to cut through between the houses and get in through his back yard, which has a big wooden fence around it, less chance of being seen that way."

"How do you know that?" I asked.

He gave me a "don't-be-stupid" look. "Because the man was my boss," he said in a too-patient voice. "He threw barbeques at his place every summer. I've been to his house before."

"Oh, yeah," I said. "I hadn't thought of that."

Stephen rolled his eyes at me.

"Can you two shut up so we can just get this over with?" Ashara said. Her voice was shaking.

"Does this scare you?" I asked, surprised.

"Yes," she said.

"Why? It's not like anyone's likely to come in and find us. The owner is in jail. Well, one of them. The other one's dead, and I don't see her suddenly showing up if she hasn't bothered to already."

"I just don't want to get caught by anyone," she said. "Do you know what happens to black people who get caught breaking and entering? They go to jail. All the time."

"We're not going to get caught," I said.

"Easy for you to say," she said. "You're white and a ghost."

"Callie's right," Stephen said to Ashara. "And if we get caught, I'll just say that Rick asked me to check up on things. He'll back me on it."

Ashara took a deep breath and nodded. "Okay. If you're positive."

"I'm positive," he said, reaching over and patting her hand.

"Hey," I said, "if you two are going to get all lovey and

shit, I'm outta here." I swung out through the back seat door and slipped between the houses until I got to Rick McClatchey's back fence. I decided to go over it instead of through it. And then I slid through the back door and into the house.

It looked a lot like it had when I had left it after Molly's death. Hard to believe that had really only been a few days ago. It seemed like months.

I turned back to the door and drew the lock. I was clearly getting better at manipulating physical objects, because the bolt slid back much more easily than I had anticipated it would.

A few moments later, Ashara and Stephen stepped up onto the back deck. I waved them in through the French doors. They had to duck under the crime-scene tape that had been haphazardly applied to it--so haphazardly that it stuck to the door frame, but not the door. *Good thing the door opens inward*, I thought.

"You know," said Ashara to me, "I'm getting used to you walking through walls. I can even deal with you showing up in the middle of trees, even though it's creepy. But watching you fly over that fence may be the most ghosty thing I've seen you do yet."

"Really?"

"Yeah. Levitation is just not normal. Don't get me wrong. I don't think that middle-of-the-tree business is all that great. But flying around with your hair all flowing out behind just ain't natural."

I stared at her for a minute. "I'm dead, Ashara. And as far as I can tell, I'm the only ghost in town. I'm not sure there's anything really 'natural' about any of this. So I'm just taking it as it comes."

She inclined her head. "There is that," she agreed.

"Can we please start doing some searching?" Stephen asked.

"Don't turn on any lights," I warned.

"Wasn't planning on it," Ashara said. "Did you hear the part about how I really don't want to get caught?"

"I've got a flashlight," Stephen said, and pulled it out of his pocket. It was one of those miniature flashlights that cast a tiny circle of light.

"Just don't use it near any windows," I said.

He nodded.

We started in the back of the house, where the McClatcheys had turned one of the bedrooms into a home office space. Stephen started with the obvious--a filing cabinet that stood in the far corner.

"Let's take the files to the master bedroom closet to look at them," I suggested. "It's huge, and no one outside will notice the flashlight if we're in there."

Stephen gave me an odd look. "You seem to know an awful lot about this house," he said. "You never did tell me how you ended up seeing Molly get killed."

If I'd had blood, I would have blushed. As it was, I could feel my eyes go all shifty. "I use to come over here on Thursdays," I said.

Stephen just looked at me, waiting for the rest of the explanation.

I sighed. "They watched *CSI*. I came over here to watch it because they couldn't see me. And because they were . . . I don't know. Nice. Comfortable. Happy."

"So you came over and watched their television and enjoyed their company?" Ashara asked.

"Yeah."

"Even though they didn't even know you were there?"

"Well. Yes."

"Okay. That may be the creepiest thing I've heard yet," Ashara said, shaking her head.

"Yeah, well, just wait until you're dead and people start peeing themselves when they see you," I muttered. "You'll start looking for some uncomplicated television-watching time, too."

"Hey," said Stephen, who had been pulling files out of the file folders. "You two want to stop talking and start helping me here?" He handed a pile of folders to Ashara, along with the flashlight. "Go on into the closet and see if any of these look promising. I'll bring some more in to you in a minute."

I followed Ashara into the closet, where she plopped down on the floor. She took a second to look around, though. "You're right. This is huge." She shook her head and started flipping through the folders, muttering to herself. "Mortgage, taxes, car loan, medical." She looked up. "All of these seem pretty standard," she said.

"Go ahead and look through them anyway," I suggested. "Sometimes things get misfiled."

Ashara shrugged and started opening the files. "Nope," she said, just as Stephen walked in and handed her another stack.

"This all looks like old college course work," she said. "Molly's. She must have been a packrat to have saved all this stuff."

We finally found what we were looking for on Stephen's fourth trip into the closet from the study.

"Hey!" said Ashara, loud enough to stop Stephen, who had started back into the study. "I think this is it. There are four different folders here labeled 'genealogy.'"

Two of the files were all about Rick McClatchey's family--copies of old letters, old photographs, marriage certificates, a carefully mapped-out family tree. The other two were devoted to Molly's family.

And there, in the middle of the second file, was what I had been hoping we would find. The birth certificate of James Powell, father of Molly McClatchey, nee Mary Powell. In the space for the mother's name was Mary Powell.

And in the space for the father's name was the name I'd been hoping to see.

Graham Howard.

One of the Howard brothers suspected of killing Mary's older brother Jimmy Powell and disposing of his body.

"I knew it!" I said triumphantly.

"You did?" Stephen asked.

"Well, yeah. You're surprised?" Ashara asked. "I thought we all knew that's what we were looking for."

"You two have got to start letting me in on the whole womanly thought process business if we're going to keep doing this detective stuff. I need to be in the loop."

"You're in the loop," I said. "You knew everything we knew."

"But that doesn't mean that I came to the same conclusions. So you've got to start discussing that part of this stuff with me. Okay?"

I shrugged. "Sure. Didn't mean to keep you in the dark."

He nodded and settled onto the floor next to Ashara.

"So what does this tell us now?" he asked.

I sat down on the floor next to them. "Okay. Jimmy comes back from the war in the forties and hooks up with the Howard brothers. They go in together and rob a bank in Atlanta--far enough away so that they won't be immediate suspects. We already know that his little sister was wild. She starts messing around with Graham Howard. At that point, I'm guessing that either Jimmy found out about Mary and Graham or that Jimmy just got greedy."

"Or both," interjected Ashara.

"Or both," I agreed.

"So Jimmy takes the money and hides it away from the Howards," Stephen said, continuing the story. "Then he and the Howards get into it and Jimmy ends up dead."

"Almost certainly," I agreed. "If he'd been alive, he would have come back for the money at some point."

"And somehow the money ends up in a safe deposit box in Mary Powell's name," Ashara said.

"Yeah. I'm a little fuzzy on that part. It's impossible to

know which Mary Powell put it there," I said.

"Not totally impossible," Ashara said. "I wasn't looking for that sort of information when I checked to see who owned the box, but I can find out when it was first rented out. That will at least give us a timeline."

"Does it really matter?" Stephen asked.

"Probably not," I said, "but I'm curious. Did Jimmy's mother know about the money? Did she put it away for her children? Or because she was ashamed? And if she was ashamed, why didn't she turn it over to the authorities?"

"I'll check it out tomorrow," Ashara said.

"Thanks," I said.

"Anyway," said Stephen, "we know that the money got put there. And sat there for we don't know how long."

"Pretty much untouched," I said. "The newspaper articles said that fifty thousand dollars went missing. That's not all that far off my guess about how much was in that safe deposit box."

"Okay," said Stephen. "Fast forward to last week. For some reason, Clifford Howard comes in and kills Molly McClatchey."

"And then," I said, "searches Rick McClatchey's house and takes a key out of a box on his dresser--almost certainly the safe deposit key. Then he goes into the bank and hands the key off to Jeffrey McClatchey, who switches the money out of Mary Powell's box into his briefcase. Then he splits the cash with Howell."

We all sat on the closet floor, staring at each other.

"If Jeffrey was already on the signature card for the safe deposit box," Stephen asked, "then why did Howard have to kill Molly?"

I shook my head. "I don't know. It doesn't make any sense."

"And another question," said Stephen. "How did Molly end up back in Abramsville? Didn't her father move to Atlanta?"

I nodded. "Yeah, he did. Good question."

"Wait," said Ashara. "I think I saw that a minute ago." She started flipping through files.

Stephen and I stared at her in confusion.

"Here it is!" she said, waving the file labeled "Mortgage." She opened it up. "When Rick and Molly got married, Molly sold the house that she'd been living in. And here's the deed to that house, which lists the owners as first Mary Powell, who passed it to James Powell, who left it to his daughter when he died six years ago."

"So she moved here because she inherited the house?" I asked.

"And probably because she could get a job teaching at the college," Stephen said. "She said once that one of the things she liked about Abramsville was that she and Rick could live well here without having to make a whole lot of money--she even mentioned that she had been able to survive pretty happily on an adjunct's salary before she met Rick."

"Which she would have done pretty quickly, since she was a music teacher and he owned a musical instrument repair shop," I said.

Stephen and Ashara nodded.

"But none of this explains why they killed her," I said. "Even if we went to the police with everything we have, we still don't have anything to connect Clifford Howard and Jeffrey McClatchey to the murder."

"I don't know," said Stephen. "The money's a pretty good motive."

Ashara shook her head. "Callie's right. It's still not enough."

We sat there, wracking our brains, coming up with nothing.

There's no telling how long we would have spent in Rick and Molly McClatchey's closet if we hadn't heard the sound of someone coming in the front door.

Chapter Nineteen

We all froze, our eyes wide.

"Wait here," I whispered. "I'll go see who it is." *And hope to hell whoever it is can't see me,* I added silently.

I crept down the hall on tip-toe. Never mind the fact that my feet weren't actually touching the floor. Creeping felt like the right thing to do.

I could hear whoever it was moving through the living room. When I got to the end of the hall, I eased my head around the corner to see if I could tell what the person was doing.

I came face to face with Jeffrey McClatchey.

It's a good thing he couldn't see me--or hear me, for that matter--because I let out a little yelp. He moved through me, then stopped and looked behind him as if trying to figure out why he'd just stepped through a cold spot. If I'd had real skin, it would have had chill bumps all over it. Brrr.

He headed down the hall toward the home office room.

"It's Jeffrey McClatchey!" I yelled out. Hey, he couldn't hear me, but Ashara and Stephen sure could. "Turn out the flashlight, be very still, and I'll see if I can distract him!"

I didn't hear any response at all. When I followed McClatchey into the office, I glanced into the bedroom and saw nothing out of place. The closet door was partly shut and the room was totally dark.

McClatchey had his own flashlight, and when he flashed it around the room, I groaned aloud in dismay. Stephen hadn't been particularly neat in his search. All the file drawers were open and it was clear that a lot of the files were missing.

"What the fuck?" muttered McClatchey. He walked over to the cabinet and fingered some of the files left behind. His eyes narrowed and he shook his head. "That son of a bitch," he said aloud.

I wondered which son of a bitch he meant. Seemed to

me there were several involved in this business. Howard seemed the most likely choice, though. Maybe McClatchey thought that Howard had come in and taken important files before McClatchey could get to them.

Or maybe he thought that his brother Rick had moved them. Or had someone come in and move them. At any rate, the fact that they were missing seemed to irritate him.

I found that comforting and happy-making. I think he deserved all the irritation he could possibly get.

And I was about to get the chance to try to add to his irritation, I saw, because he was beginning to search other places, either for the missing files or for some other item he felt he needed.

He started with the desk in the office. And as long as he stayed away from the closet in the master bedroom, I was happy to let him search. If he found what he was looking for, it might actually help answer some of the questions we still had.

He didn't so much sort through the desk drawers as dump their contents on the floor and kick them around. Whatever he was looking for wasn't there, though, if his curses were anything to go by.

Next he moved to the bookshelves and started flipping through the books. He'd take one off the shelf, flip through the pages, turn it spine-side-up, and then shake it to see if anything fell out. When nothing did, he tossed it onto the floor.

It took him about fifteen minutes to go through all the books. At one point, he took a picture of Molly and Rick off the shelf and looked at it, then muttered "Fucking nigger whore," and tossed it on the ground.

That's when I decided to start screwing with his mind even if he didn't head toward the closet.

I started with the door. It seems to be easier for me to move things that are designed with moving parts--locks, doors, those sorts of things. Much easier than, say, picking up the picture he'd just tossed on the ground and throwing it in his face--even though that's really what I wanted to do.

I gathered all my concentration and shoved at the door.

It slammed shut with a bang. *I really am getting better at this sort of stuff,* I thought.

McClatchey jumped and screamed. I giggled. He spun around and stared at the shut door. Slowly, he walked over to it and ever so carefully opened it. He poked his head out into the hallway. "Hello?" he said.

Silence.

He flashed his light into the hallway and across to the master bedroom.

Silence.

After a long, still moment, he turned back around and went back to his search. He checked the closet in the office, pulling open storage boxes and tossing their contents onto the floor. Finally, he found a small wooden box. He opened it. Inside was a bundle of what looked like old letters, tied together with a light blue ribbon that was fraying along the edges.

"Finally," he muttered, and shoved the letters the back into the box.

By this point, I had given him five or six minutes to calm down.

So I slammed the door again.

This time he froze with his back to the door.

It was almost a full minute before he turned around ever so slowly and looked at the door, his eyes huge.

"Whoever is out there, this isn't funny!" he said. "This is my brother's house and I have the right to be here. You do not. If you don't leave now, I'm calling the police."

Now that's not a bad idea, I thought.

"Hey, Ashara, Stephen!" I called out. "I'm going to keep him trapped in this room. Y'all get out of here. Take the folders with you. When you get to your car, call 911 and report strange lights flashing in the McClatchey house. As big as this case is, the police ought to come running."

Jeffrey McClatchey moved toward the door and

reached out for the doorknob. This time I pushed on it with every ounce of physical and mental strength I had. The door opened an inch and then ripped itself out of McClatchey's hand, slamming shut again. McClatchey actually whimpered.

I heard a slight scuffle as Ashara and Stephen slipped past the office and down the hall. Apparently, so did McClatchey.

"I'm calling the police right now!" he yelled.

"Yeah, right," I said aloud.

I could hear the back door open as my friends left. McClatchey, assuming that whoever had held the door shut was now gone, tried to open it again.

I didn't let him. Just for fun. And because he was a sick, nasty man who deserved to be haunted. *In fact*, I thought, *if we can't get him put in jail, I might just decide to move in with him and make his life a living hell.* I smiled at the thought.

I held the door shut on him until I saw police lights in front of the house flashing off the office window.

McClatchey saw them, too, and started to panic. First he shoved the box full of letters back into a cardboard box in the closet. Then he pulled as hard at the door as he could; it was all I could do to keep it shut until I heard police officers coming in through the still-unlocked back doors and announcing themselves.

"I'm in here!" McClatchey called out, apparently deciding to try to bluff his way through. "I'm locked in the second bedroom."

At that point I let go of the knob and stepped out of the way.

An officer, a blonde woman, opened the door easily and sighted McClatchey down the barrel of her gun. "Step out of the room, sir," she said.

"I'm Rick McClatchey's brother," Jeffrey said. "He asked me to check in on the place. And look"-- he gestured around the room--"clearly someone's been in here."

"Sir, I'm going to have to ask you to put your hands on your head and step out of the room."

"But can't you see? Someone's ripped the place apart."

"Sir, I'm only going to ask you this one more time. Put your hands on your head and step out of the room."

By now, another officer had joined her in the doorway. He put his gun away and stepped into the room, cuffs in hand. "This is an active crime scene, sir," he said. "Did you not see the crime scene tape on the door?"

"I'm telling you, I didn't do this."

"You can't be here," the second officer said, pulling McClatchey's arms behind his back and handcuffing him.

I figured I could leave them to it at this point. McClatchey didn't have a chance. So I slid out through the wall of the office and into the front yard, and then went in search of Ashara and Stephen.

I found them a block away, watching the flashing police lights in front of the McClatchey house.

"That was fun," I said, slipping into the back seat.

"For you, maybe," Ashara said. "It scared me about half to death."

"I have to admit, I had an uncomfortable minute or two there, too," said Stephen.

"But we got in, we got what we needed, and we got back out again," I said. "Mission accomplished. So we can all relax."

"Thank God," said Ashara.

"Except that we need to go back in," I said.

"What?" Ashara practically screeched.

"McClatchey found what he was looking for, but he shoved it back into place before the cops came in," I said. I described the box full of letters.

"We'll go back in and get it when the cops are gone," Stephen said. "But right now, you look like you could use some rest." I glanced down at myself. I was see-through again.

"I guess that took more out of me than I expected," I

said. "Maybe you'd better take me back to Miss Adelaide's. Or somewhere." I put my hand to my head. "I'm feeling a little dizzy right now."

Stephen got me to Maw-Maw's before I floated out of consciousness, but just barely. The last thing I remembered was sinking into the bed in the guest bedroom.

*   *   *   *

I didn't come to until mid-afternoon the next day. I was learning to loathe the fact that the only way I could deal with physical objects was to expend so much energy that I went all transparent and then passed out.

When I floated into the living room, Maw-Maw was the only one there.

"Where is everybody?" I asked.

"Ashara said she was going to work," Maw-Maw said. "And I don't know about that new white boyfriend of hers. I ain't talked to him since last night."

"He does have a name, you know," I said.

Maw-Maw cackled. "Yeah, but it sure do irritate little Miss Ashara when I take to calling him her white boyfriend."

I had to laugh at that.

"Did he have anything important to say when you talked to him last night?" I asked.

She shook her head. "Only that we wasn't going to Atlanta today 'cause y'all done found the birth certificate you was looking for."

I nodded. "Okay. I'm going to go check in with them," I said.

Maw-Maw waved her hand. "Get on with it then," she said, "and quit interrupting my stories." She turned back to the television. I got the feeling that she was more than a little disappointed that the trip to Atlanta had been canceled.

"Hey, Miss Adelaide?" I said.

"Yes?" She turned back to face me again.

"When this is all over, I think we should make Stephen drive us to Atlanta anyway. Go do something fun for the day."

She looked at me for a moment, and then smiled.

"Might be you're right, child," she said, her voice softer. Then she turned back to face the television once again and waved me off. "Now you go on and solve this big ol' crime of yours. We gots to get on with things around here, and we can't do that until them men are in jail."

Ashara was in her usual spot in the drive-through teller's window booth.

"Hey," I said, coming up behind her. "Did you and Stephen go back and get the letters?"

She didn't answer me, but she shook her head.

"What? You didn't? What if the police let him go? What if he goes back and gets them?"

"Hey, Ann," she said. "I'm going to go take a quick bathroom break, okay?"

"No problem. I've got it covered here."

I followed Ashara to the women's restroom.

"Why didn't you go back and get them?" I demanded again once we were safely locked inside.

"Because," Ashara hissed at me, "the police were there until almost midnight. And I had to get up to go to work today."

"So why didn't Stephen go?"

"Because he thought the cops might still be watching the place."

"Dammit, Ashara, those letters are clearly important."

"So is my job. So is my life. So is not going to jail, as far as I'm concerned." She was still hissing, an angry whisper. "I didn't have anything to do with this until you dragged me into it, and now I've got some crazy killer man out to get me, I'm breaking into houses late at night and almost getting caught by the crazy killer's partner, and none of this is my problem!" By the end of the sentence, she was almost yelling.

"Are you okay in there?" someone asked from outside the door.

"Just fine," Ashara said, sounding anything but.

"Look," I said, "I'm sorry. I'm really, really sorry. I'm sorry I pulled you into it. I didn't know then how bad it was going to get. But now that we're in the middle of it, we've got to see it through. If we don't, you'll be jumping at shadows for the rest of your life. Or worse, someday you'll wake up dead somewhere like me, and then you'll be sorry you didn't follow through."

Ashara grinned a wry grin at that point and rubbed her hands over her eyes. "Okay. Fine. We'll go get the letters after I get off work. Just go talk to Stephen about it."

I nodded and left the bank before she could change her mind.

Stephen wasn't in his apartment.

I found him in the workshop at Rick's store, sitting at his bench smoothing out a dent in a trombone.

"That looks like somebody stomped on it," I said.

He had been engrossed in the work and jumped a little when he saw me. He put the trombone down on his work bench and stood up. Stretching and yawning, he turned to his coworkers. "I'm going to take a break," he said.

"Fine," said the woman at the bench next to him, waving at him without looking up.

Once again, we strolled around the downtown square, this time stopping in front of a shop with lots of cute purses in the window. For a moment, I was sad about the fact that I would never have another cute purse again. I would be the eternal window shopper, but never get to buy anything.

I shook off the feeling and got down to business.

"We need to go back into Rick's house and get those letters," I said.

"I agree," said Stephen.

"So why are you at work instead of at Rick's?"

"Because Margaret called me this morning to tell me that we'd gotten a huge repair order in from the junior high school. I want to get Rick out of this, but I also want to make sure that he has some kind of life"--he paused and shook his head--"or at least a business to come back to once he gets out of jail."

I sighed. "Okay, fine. Has Jeffrey McClatchey come in to work today?"

Stephen shook his head. "Margaret says she wasn't able to get hold of him this morning."

"You think that might mean the police still have him in custody?"

He shrugged. "Either that, or he's sleeping off a long night of questioning."

"Or he went back and got those letters."

This time Stephen lifted only one shoulder. "That's a possibility, too, I guess. We won't know until we get back into Rick's place."

A woman in her fifties pulled up into a parking space behind us and got out. We both stood silent, staring at the window display, until she had gone into the store.

"Let's walk," Stephen suggested. "I've got to get back to work anyway."

"Will you go back to Rick's tonight?" I asked.

"Yes. Of course." We got to the front entrance of Rick's shop. "In the meantime," said Stephen, his hand on the door handle, "why don't you go back over there and see if you can tell if the letters are even still there."

I nodded. "Okay. Meet us at Miss Adelaide's when you're through here?"

"Sure. But it might be a little late. We've got a big job here and not much time to finish it. It's worth a lot of money to Rick. And it'll keep our paychecks coming, too, since Margaret has access to the business account."

"She does?" I asked, surprised.

"She's also the business manager here," Rick said. He pulled open the door and went inside, giving me the tiniest of waves as he headed back to the workroom.

Stephen was right. I needed to see if the letters were still at Rick's. And if they were, I fully intended to find and then follow Jeffrey McClatchey around all day long, just to make sure he didn't go back to his brother's house. And if he did, I was going to make sure he didn't get his hands on those letters.

Rick McClatchey's house was empty. I moved back to the home office, and with a great deal of effort, managed to get the lid off the cardboard box Jeffrey had shoved the wooden box into.

The wooden box was still there.

With a sigh of relief, I sped over to Jeffrey's house. He wasn't there. I spent much of the afternoon running back and forth between the two McClatchey brothers' homes; stopping in each one only long enough to make sure Jeffrey wasn't there.

Eventually, I got the bright idea of checking the local jail.

It didn't take me long to search. Abramsville's jail is tiny. But one of the drunks in one of the cells saw me flit through the bars and check the place over. I think he thought it must be part of the DTs, though, because he covered his eyes with his hands and started moaning "no, oh no," over and over again. I decided to leave him in peace, so I left as quickly as I could.

At 4:00, I went back by the bank.

"Okay, Ashara," I said. "The box of letters is still at Rick's. I'm going over to guard it. Stephen's going to meet you at your grandmother's as soon as he gets off work. I'll unlock the back door for you again. Come over as soon as Stephen comes to get you."

Ashara nodded slightly.

"Are you okay with this?" I asked.

She shook her head, and then shrugged.

"Is that a no?" I asked.

She shrugged again.

Time to play Dead Chick Twenty Questions again, I thought with a sigh.

"Is it a yes?"

She shrugged.

"Is it a maybe?"

She shook her head.

"Is it a qualified yes?"

She nodded.

"Qualified how?"

She looked up at me balefully.

"Sorry. Forgot for a minute that you couldn't answer. Um. Is it a qualified yes because you don't want to do it?"

She shrugged.

"Are you okay?" Ann asked from the next seat over.

"I've just got a little bit of a crick in my neck and shoulders," said Ashara. "Just trying to work it out." She stretched a little to demonstrate. "I'll be fine."

Ann nodded and went back to work.

"Nicely done," I said admiringly. "You're getting pretty good at hiding the fact that you're talking to an invisible person."

She rolled her eyes at me.

"Okay," I said, continuing the line of questioning. "Is it a qualified yes because you're scared?"

She nodded.

"But you're still willing to do it?"

She nodded.

I blew out a huge non-breath in a sigh of relief.

"Okay. Good," I said. "I'll see you over at Rick McClatchey's as soon as Stephen picks you up."

She nodded again.

"And be very, very careful going to your grandmother's after work. Take some weird route. Howard knows where you work and what you drive. He might be watching you. Be sure he's not following you, okay? And keep your phone out. Be ready to call 911 in case he tries to run you down again."

She stared at me, her eyes huge.

"I'm not trying to scare you. I'm trying to get you to be safe. Will you do that?"

She nodded.

"Good. I'll see you in a few hours."

I spent those hours camped out in Rick McClatchey's living room. Every so often I would go back to the office to make sure the box was still there. I've always been a little obsessive. I guess death didn't change that.

I waited until after it got dark. Finally, at almost 8:00 that evening, Stephen and Ashara came slinking up to the back deck and through the back door, once again ducking under the crime scene tape crisscrossing it.

"It's about time," I said.

"I told you it would be late," Stephen said.

"Where's this box?" Ashara said. "I want to get it and get out of here. This whole thing is freaking me out."

"It's in the office in the closet. It's sitting on top of the stuff in the cardboard box," I said.

Stephen headed to the back. Ashara waited in the living room, shifting from foot to foot.

"Did you find Jeffrey McClatchey today?" she asked. She didn't look at me when she asked the question; her eyes shifted around the room and out the back door and back around the room again.

"No," I said.

Ashara's eyes jerked to my face. "You didn't?" she asked in a horrified tone.

"No. He wasn't at work, at his house, at this house, or in the jail," I said. "And those were pretty much all the places I could think of to look."

"What about Howard's place?" Ashara asked anxiously.

"I can't go out there without your grandmother," I reminded her. "Your grandmother can't go out there without someone to drive her. And since you and Stephen both decided that it was more important to go to work today than it was to catch the killer on the loose in your hometown, I had no choice but to just wait here so that I could try to guard the letters if he came back." My voice had gone from very patient to syrupy sweet by the end of the sentence. And for anyone who doesn't know it, that tone is a big Southern "fuck you"--at least among Southern women.

Ashara, of course, recognized it for what it was.

"There's no need to get all tetchy," she said defensively. "I was just asking."

"Well, now you know," I said.

"Fine."

Stephen came back down the hallway, wooden box in hand. "This it?" he asked.

"Is it full of old letters tied with a blue ribbon?" I asked.

He flipped it open. "Yep."

"Then that's what we came for," I said.

"Good," said Ashara. "Let's get out of here now."

Stephen and Ashara moved out the back door.

"Shut it," I said. "I'm going to try to lock it again."

Stephen handed the box of letters to Ashara and pulled the door shut. I concentrated and gave a twist. The lock turned. We all headed toward the back gate in the fence, the one that led into the alley. Stephen had again parked on the block behind Rick's house. Stephen went through the gate first, and then held it open for Ashara.

At that moment, we heard an inarticulate shout from the house. Then a flashlight beam hit Ashara dead-on, illuminating her and the box she held in her hand. Ashara put her hand up to her eyes. She probably couldn't see anything, but I was off to one side of the direct aim of the beam and could tell it was Jeffrey McClatchey. He'd finally come back from wherever he'd been so that he could collect the letters.

"Run!" I yelled at Ashara.

"Hey!" yelled Jeffrey as Ashara took off through the gate. Jeffrey jumped off the deck where he'd been preparing to enter his brother's house and landed in a crouch in the grass, then straightened up to run after Ashara.

The gate was swinging slowly closed. I figured that at the speed he was running, McClatchey would have just enough time to get through it before it shut completely; he wouldn't even have to slow down to open it.

So I waited until he was almost to the gate and with a little concentrated effort, slammed it shut.

He ran straight into it at full running speed. He ran kind of like a little kid, arms pumping, and head far out in front of the rest of his body.

The impact knocked him flat. When he dragged himself back up from the ground, he was reeling. But he managed to get the gate open and start back out after Ashara.

But by the time he got to the street past the houses on the other side of the alley, Stephen's car was just pulling around a corner. I hoped McClatchey was too shaken up to take notice of anything like the license plate or make or model of the car. Or recognize it as belonging to his co-worker.

"Goddammit," he muttered, rubbing his head. A big red knot was already starting to swell up on it. *Good*, I thought. *I hope he has a concussion.*

I headed back to Maw-Maw's; hoping that what we'd gotten was worth Jeffrey McClatchey's getting a good look at Ashara.

Chapter Twenty

When I got back to Maw-Maw's, the three of them were sifting through the letters. At first, I thought, *It wasn't worth it.* The letters--at least the letters they had gone through so far--didn't tell us anything that we didn't already know.

"Dammit," I said, scanning over one of them on the coffee table. It was a love letter, barely legible, from Graham Howard to Mary Powell.

There were other letters, letters that Molly's grandmother must have saved and passed on to her own son when she died.

"This don't make much sense," Maw-Maw said, staring at Graham's letter to Mary.

"Why not?" Stephen asked.

"Well, I know that Mary was acting up and running wild, but when y'all told me Graham Howard was little James's daddy, I just thought Graham must have seen a chance and taken it. I can't believe that he was actually in love with her."

"Not enough to marry her when she got pregnant," Stephen said, disdain in his voice.

Maw-Maw shook her head. "Times was different back then, boy. It's hard enough today on a mixed couple." She gave him a significant look and then glanced over at Ashara, who studiously ignored her. "Back then, it just wouldn't have been possible. There weren't a judge in the county that would've married them. No preacher, neither. They'd have had to go up way North, and even then it wouldn't have been certain they could've gotten married. And anyway, they didn't have the kind of money it would've taken to get out of here."

"They would have after the bank robbery," Ashara said quietly.

We all stared at her.

"You think that's why they robbed the bank?"

"I think there's a good chance that's why Graham

Howard took part in it," Ashara said. "I think it might have been his plan." She was holding a letter in her hand and staring down at it. "I don't know what the other two were going to do with their share, but Graham was going to take his and run away with Mary."

"I take it that's all in that letter?" I asked.

"Yep." She set it down on the table, and then began reading it aloud, even though we could all see it.

"My dear, dear Mary," she began, her voice soft. "I's writing to tell ya that you and me is gone to get outta here together soon and go somewhere where we can married and our baby can have a proper life one with a daddy and a mamma. I got me a plan to get some money, and Owen and Jimmy is gone to help me. They don't know what the money is for, so dont go telling Jimmy. I wont tell Owen neither. I love you with all my heart. Love, Graham."

We all sat silent for a moment.

"Things sure did go wrong for those two," Maw-Maw finally said softly. "Seems a shame, don't it?"

We all nodded. Stephen took a deep breath and said, "Okay. Let's start seeing what else is in here."

We spent another half hour reading love letters from Graham to Mary, hoping for more clues but not finding them, until we came to the end of those envelopes. Underneath them were more recent letters. Maw-Maw, Stephen, and Ashara split them into three piles and began reading. I flitted around the room, trying to read over their shoulders.

Finally Ashara said, "Would you quit that, Callie? You're making me nervous. I promise we'll tell you if we find anything useful."

"Fine," I said with a huff, and sat down on the couch. Threw myself onto it, actually. So hard that my butt ended up six inches inside the cushion. I had to concentrate to lift myself out of it.

"I've got something," Stephen finally said.

"What?" I said, sliding around behind him. He set

another letter and what looked like a will out on the table.

We all crowded around it.

"Dear James," this one started in a shaky, spidery script, "I'm dying. I knows it. And I can't do nothing bout it. But I got something I need to tell you before I go. I aint got the strength to tell you this in person, but I know that you will read this letter when I go and do the right thing."

"This is interesting," I said. Everyone nodded, but no one answered. They were all too busy staring at the sheet of paper on the coffee table.

"I been keeping a secret for too many years," it continued, "And I do believe its time to tell it. My cousin Susan werent really your mamma like I always told you. My daughter Mary was. Your cousin Mary is really your mamma. I need you to know that I aint been keeping this secret for nothing all these years. I done it to protect you. I aint certain but I'm pretty sure that Graham Howard was your daddy. And I think that probably your daddy helped to kill your uncle Jimmy, the one I named you after."

"That must have been a hard thing to carry, all those years," Ashara said softly. Again, we all nodded.

"Theres more, too," the spidery scrawl continued in another paragraph. "Before your uncle Jimmy went and got hisself killed by those Howard boys, they was all friends. And he did something awful wrong with those boys. He never would tell me what exactly, but I think I know. Anyway, after he up and disappeared and I sent your mamma off stay with her cousin Susan to have you, I found a bunch of money buried out in the back yard. In my vegetable garden. Jimmy must of knowed I'd dig it up there come spring. I figure he knew he was about to get into some awful big trouble and left it there a purpose.

"I aint never done nothing with the money. Just kept it in the back yard until one year when them Howard boys come sniffing around. That was after the fuss over Jimmy disappearing died down. After that I took it to the bank and put it in one of them safe deposit boxes. Number 203 and I left the key in my top left bureau drawer. You do whatever you want to with that money. I never could bring myself to touch it. Its got your uncle Jimmy's blood on it and I cant stand the sight of it. But you use it for some good. You send that Molly of yours to college with it. She's a good girl and some good should come out of this whole thing.

"And if them Howard boys are still around after I die, you watch out for that Owen Howard. He's just as mean as a snake and twice as sneaky. His brother aint quite so bad. I think he'd of been a good man if he hadn't growed up with that mean daddy of theirs and that Owen for an older brother.

"Other than that money, I ain't got much to leave you. But the house and everything in it is yours. If your real mamma Mary comes around wanting something, you just give her whatever you think is fair. I think I'm just goin to leave that up to you."

She signed it, "All my love, Grandmamma."

The will confirmed the letter. The elder Mary Powell had left everything to her grandson James Powell. Molly's father.

At the very bottom of the box was James Powell's will. It left everything he owned to his daughter Mary, aka "Molly" Powell.

"What happened to Molly's mother?" I wondered aloud.

"She died when Molly was fairly young," Stephen said. "I remember her talking about it once."

We all sat silent for a moment.

"So how did Jeffrey McClatchey even know this box of letters existed?" Ashara asked.

"It doesn't matter," I said. "The fact that he tried to take it means that he did know about it and that means that he had motive."

"You think this is enough to go to the police with?" Maw-Maw asked.

Stephen and Ashara and I looked at each other.

"It still doesn't tie Clifford Howard into Molly McClatchey's murder," I said. "Everything we've got is good, but I still don't think it's enough."

"You don't think Howard having half the money is good enough?" Stephen asked.

I shook my head. "I don't know. It might be."

"And how are we going to prove that Jeffrey McClatchey knew about these letters?" Ashara asked.

"Well, he handled it enough yesterday," I said. "His prints ought to be all over it."

"Assuming they're not all covered up by our prints," Stephen pointed out.

"Oh, hell," I said, stomping my foot on the floor. It sunk into the carpet up to the ankle. "Why didn't any of us think to have you two wear gloves?" I demanded as I tugged my foot back out of the flooring.

Stephen shook his head. "It never even occurred to me."

"We're all new to this breaking and entering shit," Ashara said.

"Ashara," Maw-Maw said.

"I know, I know. Watch my mouth." She shook her head. "It's been a long, scary day. I'm going to go to bed. No. Wait. I'm going to make sure all the doors and windows are locked and then I'm going to bed. We can just talk about this more in the morning."

"Okay," said Stephen, "but you can't go to work tomorrow."

"Oh, not you, too," Ashara said in tones of dismay.

"Yes. Me too. Now both Howard and Jeffrey know what you look like. You are calling in tomorrow and telling them that you have. . ." he paused to think.

"The chicken pox," said Maw-Maw.

"That's good," I said. "That could keep you out for at least a week."

"But I've already had the chicken pox," said Ashara. "When I was seven."

"Does anyone at the bank know that?"

"No." Her lower lip pouted out and she scowled as she said the word.

"Good, then," said Stephen. "You call in sick tomorrow and I'll meet you here as soon as I'm done at work."

"Why do you get to go to work?" Ashara demanded, still pouting.

"Because," Stephen said patiently, "Neither Howard nor Jeffrey knows I'm involved in any of this. And if Jeffrey ever decides to come back to work, I want him to think that everything is perfectly normal. Besides, if I don't work, I don't get paid."

"I don't either," Ashara pointed out.

"Don't you lie to that boy, Ashara Jones," said Maw-Maw. "You ain't never called in sick a day of your life. You got more sick leave built up at that bank than probably anyone else there. You could be gone for weeks and you'd still get paid."

Ashara sighed heavily and closed her eyes. "Fine. I'll call in sick with the chicken pox," she said.

"Thank you," Stephen said softly. "It'll make me feel better knowing that you're safe over here."

They walked to the door together and Ashara stepped outside for a minute. When she came back in, her lipstick was smeared.

Maw-Maw and I carefully avoided looking at her, staring at the stack of letters scattered across the coffee table.

"Ashara, honey," Maw-Maw said in the most neutral voice she could muster. "Would you please put these letters back in that there box?" Ashara nodded and headed toward the table, gathering up the envelopes and beginning to stack them neatly inside the wooden box. "That is," Maw-Maw added, "if you ain't too busy thinking about that cute little white boy." She burst into peals of laughter at her own wit.

Ashara just rolled her eyes and finished clearing the table. She carefully picked up the box by the edges--"Let's see if maybe we can keep from ruining any of McClatchey's fingerprints that might actually be left," she said--and put it on the top shelf of the freezer.

"Can you think of any better hiding place?" she asked me before shutting the freezer door. "I'm too tired to come up with anything else."

"No," I said. "I think that'll be fine for now."

"Good." Ashara closed the door and headed back to what had become her bedroom, rubbing her eyes like a sleepy child. "Goodnight, y'all," she called out before shutting the door.

"Goodnight," Maw-Maw and I replied in unison.

*   *   *   *

I only drifted for a few hours that night, so I was up early the next morning. I kept trying to figure out what we could possibly come up with--other than what I suspected the police would consider ancient history--to connect Howard and McClatchey to each other.

About 6:30, Maw-Maw came grumbling out of her room.

"If you're going to stay here until this is all over," she said, "you are going to have to quit fussing about those problems so danged early in the morning."

"I didn't make a sound!" I protested.

"Don't matter," Maw-Maw said. "Just like a screeching in the back of my head, all morning long, I can hear you worrying at this thing like a dog with a bone."

I followed her into the kitchen and watched her gnarled fingers move as she put coffee on to brew.

"I'm sorry, Miss Adelaide," I said. I sank down onto a chair at the small kitchen table. "I just keep thinking there's got to be one more thing. One more piece of evidence that we could use to convince the police that Jeffrey McClatchey and Clifford Howard were both in on killing Molly McClatchey, even if Howard is the one who actually did it."

Maw-Maw nodded. "I'm sure you're right, honey," she said. "And when it's time, you'll find that last piece."

"But in the meantime, Ashara's in danger and can't go to work and Rick McClatchey is in jail for a murder he didn't commit."

"Well, I can't speak to Rick McClatchey, but it ain't going to hurt Ashara none to take a little time off and relax here with us. She ain't never even taken a vacation since she started working at that bank. She could use a day or two off."

"Are you two talking about me again?" Ashara said as she stumbled into the kitchen in her robe.

"Sure are," Maw-Maw said, handing her an empty coffee cup. "Pour yourself some of that coffee and let's go to the living room."

"Hand me that remote control, Ashara," Maw-Maw said as she settled down into her recliner. "We need something to take our minds off this murder business. Let's watch us some news and see what's going on in the rest of the world."

"I'm not sure that's going to make us feel any better, Maw-Maw," Ashara said dryly.

"Well, we won't know until we try, now will we?" Maw-Maw replied. "Now look there. An earthquake in California," she said as she changed the channel to CNN. She kept it muted, so we were just watching the images and reading the captioning below. "And mud slides," she said. "Don't it just make you wonder why those people build their houses up on those cliffs? You'd think rich people would know better than that. But apparently them Hollywood rich folks ain't got a lick of sense."

"The ones I feel sorry for are the people at the bottom of the cliff," I said.

"Oh, hell no," said Ashara. "They should know better, too."

Maw-Maw was right. This was taking my mind off our most immediate troubles. Anyway, it wasn't like there was anything we could do until Stephen came home from work. Maw-Maw couldn't drive--and neither, for that matter, could I; at least, that's what I was assuming--and Ashara couldn't leave the house. So we might as well make our own fun while we were waiting.

So there we were, cheerfully commenting on the stupidity of rich folks and the horrors of earthquakes and mud slides when suddenly, a familiar face appeared on the screen.

"Turn it up, turn it up!" I screeched while Ashara and Maw-Maw both scrambled for the remote control and an image of Jeffrey McClatchey in handcuffs marched across the screen.

We caught the reporter in mid-sentence: ". . . arrested today in connection with the murder of his sister-in-law, Molly McClatchey." A picture of Molly from happier times appeared on the screen, dark eyes and hair, sweet smile. "Police say that forensic evidence has led them to believe that Jeffrey McClatchey may have been involved in the murder. No word yet on whether Molly's husband Rick McClatchey is still considered a suspect."

The news story switched and Ashara muted the television.

"Forensic evidence," I said excitedly. "That probably means the piano wire I found in Jeffrey McClatchey's trash can at the music repair shop."

"And maybe they found his epithelials on the murder weapon," Maw-Maw said, nodding sagely. Ashara and I stared at her. "What?" Maw-Maw said. "I watch *CSI*. I know what forensic evidence means. You girls think just because you're young, you know everything. Well, I ain't lived this long just to suddenly turn stupid."

I smothered a laugh. Ashara just shook her head.

I didn't bother to remind Maw-Maw that Howard had been the one who actually killed Molly, and he had been wearing gloves the night of the murder. I didn't want to deflate Maw-Maw in the middle of her self-righteous moment.

"You know," I said. "If McClatchey's already been arrested, then there's the chance that the police are done searching his house. And they might not be looking for the same things we are. Maybe I should go over there and see if I can find anything."

"Alone, right?" Ashara asked. She sounded anxious, but I didn't think it was because she was worried about me.

"Yes," I said. "It's probably safer. Howard's still out there looking for you, and McClatchey's arrest has probably made him nervous. And we don't know if McClatchey had a chance to tell Howard anything about seeing you at Rick's. I don't want to risk Howard seeing you out. Too dangerous." I thought for a moment. "Unless I find something and need you to carry it. In which case I'll come back and get you."

Ashara sighed in relief and nodded. "You're probably right."

"Okay. So I'll go see what I can see. You wait here for Stephen. I'll come back and let you know if I find anything."

"Good luck," Ashara said as I moved out the door.

"And good hunting," Maw-Maw said.

Chapter Twenty-One

McClatchey's house was quiet. No crime scene tape or anything. It had been searched, though, and pretty thoroughly. Ransacked might be a better word. I wondered if the police had done this, or if it had been Howard, searching for the money.

For that matter, I wondered what had happened to the money, since I assumed it must have been on Jeffrey McClatchey when the police picked him up. Either that or he'd hidden it so thoroughly that no one would ever find it. If the police found it, I wondered, would they put together the same story that we had?

I began searching the place myself. Lucky for me, almost all the file cabinet drawers had been emptied onto the floor in the study, so I could peruse most of them without even having to try to move them.

Most of it was typical. Bills, flyers from stores, scraps of paper with random telephone numbers on them.

But then something caught my eye. At first, it looked like some sort of promotional flyer, a black-and-white newsprint sheet, the kind that might serve to advertise local garage sales, cars and boats and trucks for sale, that sort of thing.

Except at the top were the words "Racial Unity." The rest of the flyer was covered up by other paper.

I focused on the paper and pulled on it. Slowly, it slid across the floor and out from under the other papers. I worried for a moment about the amount of energy it was going to take to turn the pages once I got it free of the pile.

I shouldn't have worried, I quickly realized once I settled down on the floor to read it. It was awful. This was not a paper advocating unity among various races. It was a paper advocating the unity of the "Aryan" race. It was apparently the latest edition, dated for that week. The front page had two articles. Above the fold was an article on the need to prepare

for the coming race war by learning how to "live off the land."
I looked out the window at the Alabama hills in the distance.
Maybe McClatchey had been planning to retreat to the
Talladega National Forest when his sister-in-law decided "rise
up against the white man, stealing his job, raping his wife, and
killing his children." Below the fold was an article entitled
"The Villain as Hero: The Truth About Martin Luther King,
Jr." I shook my head in disgust.

*He must have just about blown a gasket when he
realized his brother was marrying a woman who was at least
half black*, I thought. *What an idiot.*

So then why wait so long to do her in? I wondered. She
and Rick had been married for several years. Then it hit me.
All of it. All at once. I had the whole story and I knew exactly
what had happened. I just had to prove it.

I flew back to Maw-Maw's house as fast as I could.

I was already talking as I came hurtling through the
door. "Ashara! Call Stephen! Tell him he has to go to
Birmingham and ask Rick what Molly was planning to do with
the money."

Ashara blinked at me, then pulled out her cell. "Okay,"
she said slowly, and hit a button.

"Miss Adelaide," I said, "I'm going to need you and
Ashara to take me out to the old Howard road just one more
time. I know it's dangerous, but this is very important."

"Well, all right, then," said Maw-Maw, and pulled
herself out of her chair. "Just let me go change out of my
nightgown and into something more presentable. Though I
don't see what you got to be in such an all-fire hurry for."

I shooed her into her bedroom, though I hated to waste
the time. If I had my way, no one was going to see Maw-Maw,
so it didn't matter how "presentable" she made herself.

Ashara held the phone out to me. "He wants to talk to
you."

I leaned in. "Hey, Stephen," I said.

"Hi, Callie. Listen, I'm in the middle of something

kind of delicate right now. Can this wait?"

"Absolutely not," I said. "This may give us enough to go to the police, Stephen. Please, please, please go to Birmingham and ask Rick about the money."

Stephen sighed. "You going to tell me what you're thinking?"

"Not yet. I don't want to influence how you question Rick about it. If I'm wrong, then no harm done. If I'm right, then we'll need to gather everything up and go to the police as soon as you get back to Abramsville."

"Okay," Stephen said. "I'm leaving now. I'll call Ashara once I've talked to him."

"Thank you, Stephen."

"Hey, I want to help." He hung up the phone with no further good-byes.

"So are you going to tell us what's up?" Ashara asked.

"Not yet. Go get dressed. I have to go out to the Howard place."

"What?" Ashara's voice went up at least a decibel.

"I'll explain later," I said.

"I haven't even showered yet," she said.

"It doesn't matter. No one is going to see you. But we need to hurry."

Ashara heaved a put-upon sigh. "Okay, fine."

I stood in the living room anxiously tapping my foot until Ashara and Maw-Maw came back out of their respective bedrooms.

"Okay," I said. "Let's go."

We all piled into Ashara's car and she backed out of the garage and down the driveway.

"Oh. And we need to stop by Jeffrey McClatchey's on our way, too," I said.

"What?" Maw-Maw and Ashara spoke in unison.

"He's in police custody. It's not like he's going to try to stop us," I said.

"Fine. I'll just be your driver and take you anywhere

you want to go without any explanation at all," said Ashara. "Driving Miss Callie."

I shook my head. "You'll understand once you see it all."

At Jeffrey McClatchey's house, I made Ashara come in and get the "Racial Unity" newspaper, expending more energy unlocking the door than I probably should have. But I had no other choice.

"What the hell is this?" she asked as she picked the paper up.

"Be careful!" I said. "There might be fingerprints on it."

"Oh, my God," Ashara said, dangling the paper from her fingertips as if it were someone else's filthy Kleenex. "Jeffrey McClatchey is, like, in the Klan or something."

"Exactly," I said. "And his brother married a woman whose father was black."

Ashara's eyes grew round. "I wonder when he found out?"

"I don't think Molly was 'passing' or anything," I said. "I think she just didn't think about it much. But it might have been a while."

Ashara nodded. "This explains a lot."

"Exactly," I said. "So now we need to go out to Howard's place so I can see if he's on the same mailing list."

Ashara gasped. "That would explain everything."

"See?" I said. "See why I'm in such a rush?"

We ran back out to the car. I didn't bother to lock Jeffrey McClatchey's door. It was just fine with me if someone decided to come in and rob him blind.

Not that that was very likely in such a small town as Abramsville.

But even dead chicks need to dream.

We parked a little ways down from our usual spot on the highway--Howard had seen that one when he helped Stephen change the tire, and we didn't want to risk him stopping by to check it out again.

"Okay," I said. "You two wait here. If you see Howard's SUV, hide. If you can't hide, run like hell. Go straight to the police station. Going past the city limits sign will snap me back to you, so you don't have to worry about me."

They both nodded, their eyes round. I'd never seen them look more alike.

I hit Clifford Howard's place at my top speed, blowing through the door so quickly that it actually rattled the screen door a bit.

He was in his usual place on the couch. He looked perfectly calm.

Good. Maybe that meant that he didn't yet know about Jeffrey McClatchey's arrest.

Loser, I thought. Then I said it aloud, just for good measure.

And I began searching. If Howard was a subscriber to the same paper, if he read it regularly, then it might still be lying out somewhere.

I just hoped it wasn't in that damned rolltop desk. I'd never find it there. And without it, it would be hard to make the connection between the two men.

It wasn't in the living room--I searched around the couch and coffee table, snarling at the murderous loser lounging on the couch every time I moved past him.

Not in the kitchen, either. I wasn't sticking my head in the toilet tank again, I decided. That had been both creepy and unnecessary last time. And besides, it would be a really strange place to keep newspapers.

And as reluctant as I was to go into the creep's bedroom, it was eventually the only place I hadn't checked.

But there it was, sitting right out in plain view on the rickety bedside table. The bastard's night-time reading material.

I nodded. Okay. That was all we needed.

I didn't even bother to try to take the newsletter. With everything we were about to give them, the police could subpoena a list of the publication's subscribers.

It was the connection we'd been looking for.

Now all I needed was to find out what Molly had planned to do with the cash.

*   *   *   *

Stephen's call didn't come until we'd been back at Maw-Maw's for over an hour.

Ashara told him what we had found and then held the phone up so I could hear him, too.

"She planned to start some sort of college scholarship fund for underprivileged kids in Alabama," Stephen said. "Anyone want to guess who she was going to name it after?"

"Mary Powell and Graham Howard," I said.

"Got it in one."

"You know what that means don't you?"

"Yep," said Stephen. "Her whole family's history was about to be made public."

"Along with the Howards' family history," Ashara said. "A history that included a Howard being in love with a black woman."

"And Molly and Rick were planning on having children sometime soon," I added. "Jeffrey McClatchey might have been able to stand his brother marrying a black woman--especially one who didn't look all that 'black'--but he couldn't stand the thought of having his family's blood mixed with hers."

"You know what this all means don't you?" Stephen asked.

"That we're going to have them arrested for murder?" I replied.

"More than that," said Ashara. "It means this can be classified as a hate crime--even worse penalties than plain old murder."

"That's right," said Stephen. He sounded especially

satisfied.

By the time Stephen pulled into Maw-Maw's driveway, we had all the information pulled together, all the evidence neatly labeled in file folders.

"I think we're ready to go to the police," I said.

"Okay," said Maw-Maw. "Let's go. I'm ready." She pulled herself up out of her chair.

"Oh," I said, dismayed. "You know what? I think it might be better if just Stephen goes."

Maw-Maw gave me a long, level look. "Because he's white?"

"Good lord," I said. "No. Because he's Rick's employee. He can say he was investigating the murder on his own because he just didn't believe Rick could do such a thing."

"Oh. Well, then. That's fine." Maw-Maw nodded, satisfied, and sat back down.

"And I'm going with him," I said. "They won't be able to see me, so I'll be able to remind him of things while he's setting it all out for them." I looked at Stephen. "Cool?"

He nodded. "Works for me."

Ashara nodded, too. "Okay. I'll stay here with Maw-Maw. Y'all come straight back here as soon as you can."

"We will." Stephen reached out and squeezed her hand.

Chapter Twenty-Two

The main desk at the local police station was manned by the same bored officer who had taken Ashara's statement just a few days ago.

He snapped to attention, though, when Stephen marched in, plopped a pile of files on the counter, and announced, "I know who killed Molly McClatchey and I've got the evidence to prove it."

The officer, taken aback, almost stammered. "The police have the investigation under control," he finally managed to spit out. But he started to reach for the files, anyway.

"No, you don't. Because you don't know everything that I know. But what I know is right here in these files." He leaned on the counter, crossing his arms over the file folders. "And as soon as you get a detective in here, I'll be happy to go over it with him." He smiled politely.

The officer stared at him for a few seconds, and then stepped away to a phone on another desk further back from the counter.

I stayed next to Stephen, but I heard a few words of the muttered phone conversation. Words like "maybe a nut-job" and "could be crazy," but also words like "but I think you ought to take a look at what he's got."

Good, I thought. *Maybe now the right men will go to jail.*

The officer returned to the counter. "Detective Green will be here in just a few moments. If you'll have a seat, he'll be happy to see you when he arrives." He gestured toward a couple of wooden benches. Stephen sat down. I floated back and forth in front of him in a sort of ghostly form of pacing.

"Don't forget to tell him about the Nazi-Aryan-white-supremacist bullshit newsletter in Howard's house," I said. "And be sure to find some way to let him know that the unidentified blood in Molly's bathroom is Howard's. Tell him you overheard it in a conversation or something. I don't know if they can use it, but you can at least get them started on figuring out a way to get a DNA sample from him. Oh. And don't forget to tell them. . ."

Stephen interrupted me--not in words, because the officer behind the counter was watching Stephen out of the corner of his eye as he ostensibly filled out paperwork. So Stephen faked a sneeze. Only it sounded a whole lot like "Shut up!"

I got the message. Dropping to the seat beside him, I said, "I just babble when I'm nervous. Sorry."

He patted the bench where my hand was, and for once I didn't mind the chill of another person's body passing through mine. He meant it to be comforting, and it was.

*   *   *   *

Detective Green came through the door looking harried. His light brown hair stood up on end as if he'd been running his hands through it all too often. The officer at the counter pointed at Stephen. Stephen stood up.

"Detective Green," the detective said, sticking his hand out.

"Stephen Davenport," Stephen said, clasping the proffered hand firmly.

"So," said Green, "I hear you have some information on the McClatchey case?"

Stephen picked up the pile of folders and handed them to Green, whose eyes widened at their heft.

"This is going to take a while, isn't it?" Green asked.

Stephen nodded. "Probably so."

"Let's go back to my desk, then."

I followed behind them. Green's desk was a clutter of paper, but he stacked it all haphazardly on one side and set the folders down in the middle of the cleared space. He gestured to a chair across from the desk for Stephen and pulled a notebook out from the middle of the now-teetering pile. He flipped it open to a fresh page and sat down, pen in hand.

An hour later, they were going back over all the details for the second--and in some cases, the third--time.

"So you started looking into this because . . ." Green trailed off.

"Because I knew Rick couldn't have been the one to kill Molly."

"And you suspected this Howard guy because you saw Jeffrey McClatchey hand off a briefcase to him."

It wasn't a question, but Stephen answered it anyway. "Yes."

"And why didn't you report this to the police?"

Stephen gave a short bark of a laugh. "Hello, officer?" he said, holding his hand up to his ear like a phone. "I just saw one guy give a briefcase to another guy. I need you to check it out."

Even Green, who was looking more and more exhausted, cracked a smile at that one.

"Okay, okay. So we wouldn't have done anything. So instead you decided to check it out yourself by breaking into a closed crime scene and two private residences."

"Yes."

"Even though you knew those were criminal acts in and of themselves."

"Yes."

"What made this so important to you?"

"Rick is my boss and my friend. He's my friend who signs my paycheck. He goes to prison, I lose my job. And he didn't do it."

Green nodded. "Tell me again about the money."

"I think it came from a 1940's bank robbery in Atlanta. Fourth Federal. If you run a check on the serial number of the five-hundred-dollar bill in there, I think you'll see I'm right."

Green pulled the bill out and looked at it appraisingly.

"And Howard and McClatchey arranged to kill Molly and frame her husband in order to get the money and keep it from becoming general knowledge that Molly was part black."

"Yep. That's it."

"Because Molly was going to set up a scholarship in her grandparents' names?"

"Yes."

"Why didn't she just give the money back to the bank?"

"Rick says she checked into it. The bank was insured and paid back long ago. No one lost their life savings from it. The statute of limitations had run out on the robbery." Stephen shrugged. "Rick said that Molly wanted to put the money to good use."

Green leaned back in his seat. "How do I know you didn't kill her off to get the money? How do I know that you aren't just coming in here to frame them? Or just to save your boss because you've got a beef with his brother? You two are co-workers, right?"

Stephen laughed again. "You've got all the evidence I have. It's right there in the folders. And you were already suspicious of Jeffrey McClatchey, or you wouldn't have arrested him this morning. All you have to do is make the connection between McClatchey and Howard by getting the list of subscribers to that newsletter. And if you can find McClatchey's half of the cash, it would be even better. Last I saw, Howard's half was in the rolltop desk in his living room."

"So tell me again: why didn't you take the newsletter from Howard's home?"

"Because I didn't know it was important at the time. I grabbed the bill from the rolltop desk and saw the publication, but didn't realize it could connect him to Jeffrey."

Green shook his head. "You're not telling me the whole truth," he said, his eyes narrowing.

Stephen sighed. "What else can I do to convince you?" he asked.

Green leaned forward intently. "Give us a DNA sample."

Stephen stared at him, confused.

"Oh!" I said excitedly. "They're trying to figure out where that extra blood drop came from. It's Howard's. Say yes, Stephen, say yes!"

"Okay," said Stephen, shrugging. "Sure."

Green tilted his head and looked at Stephen thoughtfully. "You know this might place you at the crime scene."

Stephen shook his head. "Not possible. You might find something in the study where I searched for the files, or the master closet where I hid to go through them, but you're not going to find anything around where Molly was killed. Or . . ."--he paused, reluctant to say the word--"or dismembered because I wasn't there."

Green picked up the phone and made a call, asking someone to bring over a DNA swab kit. Then he turned back to Stephen. "You know what?" he said. "I actually believe you. I believe everything you've told me. But there's something important you're leaving out." He shook his head. "And whatever it is, it's important to you. And that makes me suspicious."

"Make it about Ashara," I suggested.

Stephen chewed on his bottom lip and looked at the ground, as if trying to decide whether or not to answer. Hell, for all I knew, he really was trying to decide whether or not to answer. I'm sure he didn't really want to drag Ashara into this if he could avoid it.

Finally, his shoulders slumped for a second, and then he took a deep breath, preparing himself to speak.

"My girlfriend was with me for some of this," he said. "I didn't want to drag her into it, in case I got in trouble for the breaking and entering."

Girlfriend, I thought. *He's calling her his girlfriend now. Interesting.* I'd have to pass that little tidbit on to Maw-Maw at some point when the other two weren't around.

"What's your girlfriend's name?" he asked, pen poised over the paper.

"Ashara Jones," he said.

Green made a note.

"Tell him that Howard knows about Ashara," I urged.

"Actually," said Stephen, "there should already be a report on file. Clifford Howard saw her at one point, and he's been kind of following her around. She came in a few days ago and reported him trying to run her off the road."

Green looked at him hard. "A man you suspected of brutally killing Molly McClatchey has been after your girlfriend and you just now come in to tell us about it all?"

Stephen shook his head. "You wouldn't have believed us before. We didn't have enough evidence."

Green nodded--almost unconsciously, it seemed--and began flipping through the files. He picked up Mary McClatchey's letter to her grandson James. He read through it, nodding again.

"Okay," he said. "Wait here for a moment."

He stood up and headed toward the back of the office, where he pulled a file out of an enormous filing cabinet.

He came back and sat down, flipping the file open in front of Stephen.

In it were full-color pictures of the crime scene. On the top of the stack was one of Molly, lying in a pool of blood, her joints separated from each other by inches.

Stephen's face blanched, and he swallowed convulsively. "Oh, God," he said, and closed his eyes, turning his face away from the photographs.

"If you're right, this is the monster who's been chasing your girlfriend," Green said. "You should have come to us earlier."

"She tried," Stephen said, meeting Green's eyes squarely and avoiding looking at the picture. "She put in a report that the guy tried to run her down." His voice grew angry. "No one followed up on it. No one from this station even called her. No one."

Green nodded and flipped the folder closed again.

"Point taken."

He moved away from the desk again to put the folder back in its drawer. On the way back, he stopped at a phone and made another call.

He leaned back in his seat again, tapping his desk. "Someone will be here in a few minutes to take that DNA sample."

Stephen nodded. "Fine. But you might want to take a sample of Howard's DNA while you're at it."

Green smiled. "Oh, we'll get to that. But we might have to have to get that subscribers' list before we'll have enough for a warrant. I've got a call into a judge right now. We'll see what he thinks."

At that moment, I started getting a strange feeling in my middle. A rubber-band feeling.

"Oh, shit," I said. "Something's wrong. Maw-Maw's--" and then *pop!* I was no longer in the police station.

For a moment, I wasn't entirely sure where I was. It was dark, and I was bouncing around a lot. Then I realized I was in the back seat of Jeffrey Howard's SUV. Clifford Howard was driving, gripping the wheel tightly and staring at the road intently.

I heard a moan come from behind me. I turned around to see Maw-Maw and Ashara, both lying in the back of the SUV, their hands bound behind and tied to their feet by a running rope--*hog tied*, I thought in horror, remembering the rodeos I'd gone to when I was still alive in Texas. Their mouths were covered by strips of duct tape.

And I had no way to get back to Stephen to tell him what had happened.

Chapter Twenty-Three

Oh, God. I may have just thought it, but I may have said it aloud. At any rate, Ashara's eyes snapped up to mine and I saw hope in hers.

I had some hope, too, but it all depended upon Stephen being able to figure out what had happened. He knew I was tied to Maw-Maw, knew Maw-Maw and Ashara had agreed to wait for us to come back to Maw-Maw's. He had to know something was wrong.

He even knew that Jeffrey McClatchey had been arrested and that we had been worried about Howard freaking out over it.

Stephen's smart, I thought. *I just have to trust that he'll find us.*

And in the meantime do everything I could to try to get Maw-Maw and Ashara away from Howard.

The feeling in the pit of my non-corporeal stomach now wasn't rubber-band-ish. It was terror. The sort of terror I hadn't experienced since before I died. I felt paralyzed, unable to act, much as I had felt when that son-of-a-bitch freakazoid in Dallas had me tied up in his basement, playing with me for day after day after day.

And I had watched Howard cut Molly into pieces. I knew what this man was capable of. I knew he was going to kill Ashara and Maw-Maw.

My mind kept repeating over and over, *This is not happening.*

But it was. *Snap out of it, Callie*, I told myself harshly. *You're not tied up here. And you do have some abilities. Think, girl. Think.*

Okay. I knew how to fiddle with electricity. I'd already fritzed this SUV out once. Maybe I could do it again.

I moved up into the passenger seat, and concentrated on the panel. I touched it, imagined energy coursing through my palm and into the wires, and the entire panel, along with the headlights, flashed, sputtered, then died. But the car kept running.

"What the fuck?" Howard said, fiddling with the controls.

Then he shook his head and kept driving.

I tried to remember what I had fried out in the engine before. Maybe if I concentrated on that, it could make the SUV stop running. Not that it had kept Howard from fixing it last time. But maybe this time it would give us enough time for Stephen to find us.

But it didn't work. Maybe I had to have my hand closer to it--on the hood or something--to short it out. Either that or maybe I wasn't remembering the right thing. It's not like I knew much about cars.

Okay, then, if not the car, maybe I could get Ashara and Maw-Maw untied. I moved to the back, settling between them.

I started with Ashara, concentrating on the rope around her hands. But when I pulled on it, it tightened the rope around her ankles, forcing her to bend her knees up further behind her.

The road suddenly got bumpier, and I turned around to look. We were on the old Howard place road.

At least he's taking us to his house, I thought. That'll be the first place Stephen will think to look.

But then, a few moments later, we left the road, passed the house, and went driving across a field behind the Howard farmhouse. In moments, we were on a small dirt track running among trees and underbrush. A track that wasn't easily visible from the house, especially not after dark. Ashara and Maw-Maw were being bounced around unmercifully, unable to brace themselves in any way.

I slammed my fist into the seat back in front of me, then pulled it out of the leather. I couldn't think what to do.

This is worse than my own death, I thought. I knew I was trapped then, that there was no getting away from the psychopath who had caught me. This time, I should have been able to do something. But I couldn't even go back and tell Stephen where we were.

Howard seemed to know exactly where he was going, despite the lack of headlights on his car. He finally came out of the woods and into a large clearing. An old, tumble-down barn sat in the middle of the clearing, probably a relic from a time when the Howard place had been a working farm.

He pulled to a stop in front of the barn, and got out to open one of the barn doors. The inside was actually better preserved than I would have guessed from the outside appearance. He'd clearly used this barn for something before.

I shuddered to think what that might be.

Howard came around to the back and popped open the hatch of the SUV.

Now's my only chance to see if I can get back to Stephen, I thought. *I know where they are. Maybe I can tell him.*

And with any luck, he would have figured out that something was seriously wrong and gotten the police headed toward Howard's place.

I set out toward town full speed ahead, scanning the highway for the cavalry. But there were no flashing blue and red lights, no sirens wailing, and no police cars screaming down the road. Not even Stephen's little car.

I stopped right outside the city limits, scanning the road ahead for anything. Any sign of help. But I saw nothing other than the occasional car passing by, going the speed limit.

Nothing to give me any hope whatsoever that help might be on the way.

With a deep un-breath, I stepped out past the city limits. It was the fastest way to get back to Maw-Maw and Ashara and sure enough, *pop!* and I was back on the old Howard farm--inside the barn, this time. I could tell that it had held horses at one time--stalls lined the outside walls of one side. And I'd been right. The interior was fairly well maintained.

Howard was in one of the stalls, muttering to himself. He had been prepared for Molly's murder--he, or he and Jeffrey McClatchey--had planned it out carefully. But this wasn't something he had planned. It was spur-of-the-moment, and he was having to improvise.

Still, not too bad for improvisational kidnapping, I thought. Ashara and Maw-Maw were both still tied up, though he had changed the configuration of their ropes. Maw-Maw sat on the ground, her hands tied behind her back; her feet stretched out in front of her and tied at the ankles. Ashara's hands were stretched high above her, tied to a hook sticking out of the wall, the sort of hook I'd seen ranchers at home in Texas hang saddles and other horse-riding gear on. Her feet, also tied at the ankles, barely brushed the ground, so that she was forced to carefully balance on her toes to avoid dangling. *Her shoulders have to ache like hell already*, I thought. Both of them still had duct tape across their mouths. I moved to stand between them, brushing my hands across their shoulders, feeling helpless and angry.

Howard stood a few feet away, examining them thoughtfully.

"So," he said, "should I kill grandma first and then do you," he asked, aiming his question at Ashara, "or should I make grandma watch me fuck you first?"

Neither woman moved. They just glared at him. I realized anew that they had the exact same eyes and the exact same facial expressions.

Howard tapped his finger against his lip, considering.

"Yeah. You first," he said to Ashara, smiling a hard, ugly smile. "Grandma ought to get a kick out of watching. I know I would."

Maw-Maw's eyes narrowed as she watched him move into one of the stalls. When he came out with a knife, she began wiggling, determinedly inching herself closer and closer to Ashara, as if she might be able to stop him somehow.

I focused all my attention on the hook, pushing and

pulling as hard as I could, hoping to pull it out of the wall, to distract Howard. Anything. Nothing happened.

"Fight back, Ashara," I said desperately. "Do whatever it takes to keep him off you." Yeah. Like I was one to talk. I'd fought back with everything I'd had, and look where I was now. Dead in Alabama, unable to keep my friends from having to go through the same horrors I had endured at the end of my life.

As he came toward her with the knife, her eyes widened and she began to thrash wildly.

Howard's smile turned evil. "Oh, don't worry, baby," he said in a crooning voice, "I'm not going to cut you. Not yet." He reached out with the knife and slashed the front of her shirt open, leaving it hanging open, exposing her bra and skin.

"Now," he said, "I suggest you stay very, very still. I don't want to cut you by accident." He reached for her pants and sliced them away in a surprisingly delicate and deft motion. Ashara stayed completely still during the operation, an occasional whimper escaping her throat.

"Good girl," he whispered, his voice throaty. His hands went to his own pants and I saw with horror the growing bulge in them. He took a step closer to Ashara.

"Rack him," I said suddenly. Ashara looked at me, her eyes wild and uncomprehending. "He's going to have to untie your legs to do what he wants to do." I spoke quickly, hoping to break through the terror I saw in her face. "When he gets close enough, swing your legs up and hit him in the balls. It'll slow him down."

Ashara took a deep breath, nodding. Howard, his pants now on the dirt floor, took another step toward her. His penis stood erect and purple and for a moment I wished with all my heart that I could use the knife on him.

Ashara swung herself backwards as if to try to move away from him.

"Good," I said.

And then she used the momentum she'd gained to

swing her legs up. Pulling her knees into a crouching position, she slammed them straight into his groin with every ounce of force she could muster.

He dropped instantly, clutching himself. He couldn't even take a breath. Ashara used that time to swing herself back and then forward again to kick him in the head--not once, but twice.

Maw-Maw nodded in approval.

Howard rolled away, groaning.

I used the time to pull at the hook again. This time it loosened ever so slightly. But it was going to take me hours to get it completely loose, and I didn't have hours.

Howard stood up again and moved in again toward Ashara, the knife held out in front of him. It was the only thing standing up in front of him, I noticed with satisfaction.

"You fucking nigger bitch," he said. "You're going to pay for that." He slashed at her face with the knife. She whimpered, and a line of red opened up on her cheek. Blood dripped down her face.

"Don't move," he said, "or it'll be worse." Ashara stayed perfectly still. Howard nodded in satisfaction, then reared back and slapped her across her cut cheek. Blood flew in droplets across the room, soaking instantly into the dirt floor, leaving dark brown spots on the red Alabama dirt.

Howard pulled a handkerchief out of his back pocket and tied it tightly around Ashara's neck. She gasped for air, and I could hear the wheeze as she struggled to breathe.

"Don't worry, sweetheart," he said. "I hear it makes everything hotter." He leered at her. Then he bent down to cut the rope holding her ankles together, pulling her legs apart and moving in between them. He slipped the knife under her bra and sliced it open.

I heard Maw-Maw behind me groan past the tape across her mouth. She moved in closer behind me, and I could virtually feel the anger coming off her body in waves of heat.

And then it hit me. I could feel her anger. Not virtually.

Really. That was really heat against my non-existent back.
Anger. Anger is energy.
And energy was the one thing I knew I could use.
I didn't know if I could use it to do what I wanted to
do.
But I could sure as hell try.

Chapter Twenty-Four

I put my hand down on Maw-Maw's shoulder. And this time, I really felt her shoulder. My hand didn't slip into her like it usually did.

Then I reached out until I could cup Ashara's cheek, the one Howard had cut.

"Look at me, Ashara. Look at me. Come on, honey." Ashara rolled her eyes toward me. "That's good. You're going to be okay, sweetheart. You're going to get through this. I want you to keep looking at me. And I want you to think about how mad you are."

Her eyes shone with fear.

"No, Ashara. Don't think about being scared. Think about how mad you are. How angry you are that he's got you tied up, that he's treating you like an animal."

Her eyes narrowed.

"That's it," I said.

I could almost see Ashara's anger well up around her, surrounding her in a red haze.

"Good, that's right, Ashara."

Behind me I felt Maw-Maw's angry heat. And I opened myself up to them.

Howard had used the time to move up between Ashara's legs. He dropped her left leg so that he could reach up and grab her breast.

An angry noise escaped her. Howard leered at her. "You like that?" he asked. "Huh? You like that, you nigger bitch? Well, you're gonna like this even more." He let go of her breast to tug at his penis, clearly recovered from the earlier shock of Ashara's kick to the groin.

I imagined pulling, tugging Ashara's anger into me, then Maw-Maw's. And I remembered what the son of a bitch who had killed me had done to me beforehand. And I felt the anger-energy slide into me. Just when I felt that I couldn't hold any more, that the anger of three people was somehow going to spill out of me, I saw my body begin to glow.

Apparently, so did Howard.

"What the hell is that?" he asked, letting go of himself.

I gave a mental push, shoving every bit of concentration into my own incorporeal body.

Howard took a step back from Ashara.

I looked down at myself and realized for the first time since my death what I must have looked like the day they found me.

My clothes were in tatters, sliced away with a box-cutter. A slit in my stomach dripped blood down my already-bloody legs. Shiny visceral glints showed through various cuts.

I took a step toward Howard, holding out my arm, pointing at him with my index finger. Blood dripped off the end of the finger where the nail should have been, and I remembered that the son of a bitch had pulled them out. For fun. The blood didn't hit the ground--it was as incorporeal as the rest of me--but it certainly had an effect on Howard.

He fell backwards, scuttling away from me like a crab as fast as he could go.

"Let them go," I said as loudly as I could. I had read the word "sepulchral" before, but never actually experienced it. But that's how my voice sounded now, deep and sonorous, as if it were echoing from some deep grave. I sounded like I belonged in a Gothic novel. It was kind of cool.

Howard cowered where he had run out of scuttling space, up against the wall of the barn. I lifted my feet off the ground and floated until I was hovering over him. I leaned down, putting my face close to his. I didn't know what my face looked like, but if I remembered correctly--and if Howard's expression were anything to go by--it wasn't pretty.

"You're going to die a slow death," I whispered in my ugliest voice. "A slow, painful death. You're going to hurt and bleed and pray for death before it comes to you and when it does, you'll wish it hadn't. Because you're going to hell."

Like I was one to make such a prediction. The living might not know jack about the dead, but I don't know jack about any afterlife other than mine. I don't even know if hell existed. But in Howard's case, I sure hoped it did. And apparently, Howard bought what I was saying; he covered his head with his arms and started whimpering. I guess a bloody, sliced-up corpse of a ghost is a pretty convincing when it comes to predictions about hell.

And that's when I almost did it.

I almost killed him.

I took my hand and I slid it right into his chest, ignoring the shock of cold that slammed up my arm. Like I said, it's pretty cold on this side, too. I used my arm as a lever to pull him up to his feet.

His face went white, all the blood running out of it as he looked down at my cold, cold hand stuck in the middle of his body.

I could feel his heart. I could feel its panicky, butterfly beating, first steady, then faster, then fluttering in odd rhythms. I ran my finger over the left ventricle--if my memory of high school biology serves--and watched his face turn gray.

I'm going to give this man a heart attack, I thought. Truth be told, I almost didn't care.

But I couldn't untie Ashara and Maw-Maw by myself. And ultimately, when it came right down to it, I wasn't a killer. It wasn't up to me to exact vengeance.

Even if I was a ghost with super-creepy killer powers.

So I pulled my hand back out of his chest. He collapsed to the ground, whimpering and panting.

"Untie them," I said, pointing at Ashara and Maw-Maw.

He pulled himself up to his feet and staggered back over to them. He untied Ashara first, pulling her bound hands off the hook and then shakily untying the knotted rope around her wrist. She gulped at the air, gasping when he removed the bandanna from around her throat. As soon as she could, she jerked away from him and pulled the duct tape off her mouth. She glared at Howard, and then spat in his face.

"Pick up the knife, Ashara," I said, "and cut your grandmother free."

Howard watched them with hate in his eyes, his color slowly returning. I drifted up behind him, whispered in his ear.

"Don't even think about it," I said. I could see the coolness of my breath as a mist in the air by his ear. I ran my hand along his shoulder, letting it sink in just a freezing inch or so. He shuddered and stepped back away from all of us.

Ashara finished removing the ropes from Maw-Maw and helped her to her feet.

I moved around to face Howard.

"Run," I said. I smiled evilly as I said it. "Run as fast and as far as you can and maybe I won't find you."

His eyes grew huge.

"But then again," I said, running a cold, dead, bloody, fingernail-less finger across his cheek, "maybe I will."

He whimpered a final time, and then bolted for the door.

A few seconds later, we heard a car door slam and the engine of the SUV rev up as pulled away from the barn just as quickly as he could.

"Why the hell did you do that?" Ashara asked. "Now he'll get away!"

I shook my head. "No, he won't. Because you're going to get yourself to his house and call 911 and I'm going to follow him. The police will pick him up."

"I'm proud of you, girl," Maw-Maw said, looking at me.

"Of me? Why?"

"For not killing that man. He sure deserves it, all right, but you're right to leave it up to God." She smiled wryly. "Or at least the state of Alabama."

I wasn't sure that was what I had done, but still, I felt Maw-Maw's pride as a glow in the center of my being.

A very different kind of glow from the one I had been emitting when Howard was in the room. That glow was fading now, and when I looked down, I looked like I had always looked to myself. Non-bloody. With fingernails. I preferred it that way, really. If I have to be a ghost, at least I'm not an All Creepy, All The Time kind of ghost.

This also probably meant that I could follow Howard again without him knowing I was there.

I left the barn to catch up with him. Ashara and Maw-Maw limped out after me, leaning on one another.

Chapter Twenty-Five

I met Stephen about a mile outside the city limits. Howard had gone straight toward town, pushing the SUV as hard as he could, even without any headlights or interior dashboard monitor lights.

But he still wasn't as fast as I was. He was still behind me when I dove into Stephen's car head-first through the windshield and landed with my head stuck halfway through the passenger seat. My butt was up in the air, my legs still outside the car.

I popped my head up out of the seat and said, "Howard. Headed this way. No headlights. Stop him."

Stephen stomped on the brake and screeched to a halt, the car spinning halfway around on the highway.

"Everyone okay?" he asked. His voice was trembling.

"Safe. Alive. As well as could be expected," I said. "That's him. Here he comes."

"Hold on," Stephen said. His car was already sideways in his lane, so as Howard got close, he simply hit the gas.

Stephen's little Honda slammed into the side of the SUV so hard that it sent me flying out the windshield. Lucky for me I was already dead.

Lucky for them that both Howard and Stephen were wearing seat belts and had air bags.

I checked on Stephen first. He was shaken, but otherwise unhurt. And angry enough that the adrenaline helped push him out of his destroyed car and up to the driver's side of the SUV. The back passenger door was smashed in to the middle of the seat. If Stephen had hit the gas just a second earlier, the impact would have been on the driver's side door and probably would have killed Howard. I wondered for a moment if that's what Stephen had been hoping for. But then I decided that I didn't care.

Anyway, who was I to talk? I'd stuck my hand in his chest and just about given the man a heart attack. Why should

Stephen feel any less vengeful?

At any rate, he hadn't killed Howard. He'd knocked him out, though. And Howard's air bag had burst, leaving a nasty chemical burn on one side of his face.

Good, I thought. I mean, I might not want to be the one to kill him, but I had no problem with him suffering a little.

Stephen dragged Howard's inert body out of the SUV and dropped it to the ground, where he started kicking the man in the ribs, over and over. "Wake up, you fucking asshole!" he screamed. "Wake the fuck up!"

It took me a long time to break through Stephen's rage. But I repeated his name over and over, until finally he looked up at me, breathing hard. "What?" he said, anger still clouding both his voice and his eyes.

"Look at me, Stephen."

"What?" He reared back to kick Howard again.

"Stephen Davenport!" I yelled this time. He dropped his foot to the ground and looked at me. "Call 911. Tell them that you've just caught Clifford Howard and that they need to send Detective Green. And that they should send one ambulance here and another ambulance to the Howard place. Give them careful directions."

"An ambulance to the Howard place?" he repeated frantically, his eyes growing huge.

"Ashara and Maw-Maw are okay. They've just got a few minor cuts and bruises. But they've been traumatized. They need to be looked at."

"Cuts?" His eyes clouded over with anger and he kicked Howard again, this time in the head.

Howard moaned.

"Stephen! 911! Now!" I barked.

He took a deep breath and nodded. He pulled his phone out of his pocket, his hand shaking.

By the time he was done talking to the 911 operator, his voice was shaking, too. I thought he might be going into shock.

"Okay," I said. "Before you collapse, you need to tie Howard up. See what he's got in the back of his truck."

Stephen shook his head. "I've got something," he said. He went around to the trunk of his car and came back with a package of guitar strings.

He rolled Howard over roughly on the pavement, prompting another moan from the unconscious man, then tied his hands together so tightly with the strings that they quickly turned purple.

I didn't mention it. I suspect that if Stephen noticed, he didn't care.

Then Stephen got a couple of flares out of his trunk and set them up around the crash site.

Several cars drove by, creeping around the wreck, but not stopping to help. The sight of the man face down on the pavement with his hands tied behind his back might have had something to do with that, but I'm not sure.

*   *   *   *

The state patrol officers were the first on the scene, actually, two cars. Either they'd gotten the 911 call or a passing motorist had called to report the accident. Or both.

Ashara had beaten Stephen to the call. She and Maw-Maw were still at the Howard house.

The first officer looked from Howard's body to Stephen, his eyes narrowing in confused suspicion. "You want to tell me what's going on here?"

"Hang on, baby," he said to Ashara. "I've got to talk to the police. We'll be there soon. Call me back in ten if you haven't heard anything." He disconnected. "Sure," he said, turning to the officer. "I'll be happy to tell you what happened. This man is Clifford Howard. He's wanted in connection with the Molly McClatchey murder. And he kidnapped my girlfriend and her grandmother. That was her on the phone-- my girlfriend, not her grandmother. She's at this guy's house. She just called 911, too."

The officer turned around to the other cop on the scene,

who nodded and went back to his car; presumably to check with dispatch to see if such a call had indeed come in.

"Ask for Detective Green," Stephen called after him.

The first officer scratched his head and looked down at Howard, who was beginning to regain consciousness and was moaning even louder than before.

"Well, let's at least put some regular cuffs on him," he said. He reached into his pocket and pulled out a knife. Snapping it open, he cut through the guitar strings. Howard's hands twitched as the blood ran back into them, and he moaned again.

The officer cuffed him.

"So tell me how this accident happened."

Stephen took a deep breath. "Well, it wasn't so much an accident," he said.

The policemen gave him a level look. "Then tell me how this wreck happened."

"Okay. I knew that Clifford Howard had my girlfriend. So when I saw his SUV, I rammed it."

"You weren't worried that your girlfriend might be in the car and that you might injure her?"

"I wasn't really thinking that clearly," Stephen said.

The second officer came back. "His story checks out," he said. "Green's on the way."

At that moment, Howard woke up and started screaming. "She's coming after me!" he said, his words a long wail.

"Who is?" the second officer asked.

"Oh, God," Howard wailed. "She's dead, and cold, so cold. My heart. She touched it. And she's coming. I have to run. You have to let me go."

"Who's dead?" the officer asked.

"The bloody woman. Oh, God, let me go." Howard pulled at the handcuffs. "You've got to let me go. She'll get me otherwise. Let me go."

Stephen looked at me through narrowed eyes, and then

turned so that his back faced the officers. "What did you do?" he mouthed more than whispered.

"Long story, I'll tell you later," I said.

Stephen shook his head and turned back to the policemen.

The first officer shook his head, too. "This is going to be a long night, isn't it?"

"But at least all we've got to deal with is the wreck. We can hand the rest of it over to Green," his partner replied.

"Thank God. This looks like the kind of mess I want to stay out of."

*   *   *   *

In the end, though, he didn't get to stay out of it. Because Howard lived outside the city limits, and because the McClatchey case was so very high-profile, pretty much all the cops in the county got in on the action.

Howard got dragged off to the hospital, complete with police escort. Both Howard's SUV and Stephen's Honda got towed away--taken, I suspected, to some lab where they would be gone over with a fine-tooth comb. And fingerprint powder. And probably some other cool CSI-type stuff.

Green had eventually taken Stephen out to the Howard place with him, but only after Stephen threatened to walk if Green didn't give him a ride.

"You need to get checked out," Green said.

"Fine. There will be an ambulance out there, too," Stephen said.

Green sighed. "Okay, okay. But only because you were right on this one and I was wrong."

Once we got out to the Howard place, I pulled Stephen aside long enough to ask him what had happened after I popped out of the police station."

"I told Green that I was worried about Ashara, so I started trying to call her. She didn't answer, of course, so I got even more worried. Green wasn't buying it--he said that she probably had the phone turned off. So I told him I was going to check on her. He told me not to leave town, and then went back to reading the stuff in those files. Pissed me off, but there wasn't much I could do about it."

"Well, you stopped Howard, and that's what counts."

"Yeah, but not before he got to her."

"He didn't get to her too much, Stephen. I made sure of that."

"You?"

"Yeah. I'll tell you the story sometime."

He was still looking at me incredulously when Green came over and said, "Okay. I've got a few more questions for you, and then you can go talk to your girlfriend."

I figured that was my cue to leave.

*   *   *   *

An hour later, we all sat huddled together in the open back door of an ambulance: me, Ashara, and Maw-Maw. Maw-Maw and Ashara had each been taken aside for private questioning and then brought back to the ambulance, where an EMS tech had checked them over. Now the police were once again questioning Stephen about his role in the evening's events.

A balding, rotund policeman came over to the ambulance. "And what was your part in this, ma'am?" he asked.

"I already told that detective over there," Ashara said irritably, pointing at the first man who had questioned her.

"Not you," he said to Ashara. "You."

I realized he was talking to me.

Oh, hell and damn. The cop could see me. Fabulous.

"I'm just a friend," I said. "I'm in town visiting Ashara and Miss Adelaide. They called me after they called 911."

"So you weren't here during the events of the evening?"

"No, sir."

"What's your name?"

"Callie Taylor," I said, surprised into giving him the

truth.

"Where you visiting from?"

"Dallas." There. Let him go run a check on me now. Callie Taylor, victim of a serial killer. That ought to blow his mind.

"Do you have any I.D. on you?"

I shook my head. "No, sir, I didn't think to grab my purse before heading out here. I was in a bit of a hurry."

"How did you get here?" he asked, looking around. There were a lot of police cars and a couple of ambulances in the dirt driveway, but that was it. No other visible means of transportation. And Stephen wouldn't know to tell anyone that he'd brought me. Not that anyone else would ask. This cop seemed like the only one who was at all aware of my presence.

"I hitched a ride," I improvised.

"Hitched?"

"Yeah." I grimaced. This wasn't going to go over well. Then again, neither would this cop's report on the activities of a woman that no one else had seen at the crime scene. Oh, well. "I walked to the highway and stuck my thumb out. A trucker saw me and pulled over. He was nice enough to give me a ride to the end of the road. I walked from there."

"Did you get the trucker's name?"

"Yes, sir. John."

"Last name?"

"He didn't say."

The cop looked at me suspiciously. I didn't know if it was just a general sort of suspicion, the sort that all policemen seem to develop eventually, or if he really wasn't buying my story. I just kept my mouth shut, deciding that silence was the better part of valor at the moment--or something like that, anyway.

"Hitchhiking is dangerous," he finally said. "Not to mention illegal. You could have ended up in a lot of trouble."

I nodded, tried to force a note of sincerity into my voice. "Yes, sir, it's not the sort of thing I usually do. But this seemed like sort of an emergency." I tried to sound contrite.

He nodded, apparently satisfied.

"Well, don't do it again."

"No, sir," I said. "I won't."

He wandered off in search of something else official to do.

Maw-Maw let out a snort. "Think he's going to include that in his report?" she asked.

"Oh. Almost certainly," I said. And then the three of us started howling with laughter. I don't think it was so much that we thought the policeman's impending discomfiture was all that funny, really--though it did have an element of humor to it. I think it was more a release of tension.

We'd made it through the night, and the bad guys were going to jail.

That deserved a huge belly laugh, in my opinion.

We'd finally almost quieted down when Stephen walked up to the ambulance.

"What's so funny?" he asked.

That sent us into peals of laughter all over again.

Finally Ashara caught her breath. "We'll tell you later, honey." And then she leaned over and kissed him for a long time, over and over again.

Maw-Maw and I smiled at each other over their heads.

Epilogue

So I didn't get my angel's wings for uncovering the secret behind Molly McClatchey's death and making sure the right men were behind bars. No bells rang, no stars twinkled in the night. It may be a wonderful life, but I'm no Clarence. Like I said, the living don't know jack about the dead.

But it's actually turning out to be an okay un-life. Maw-Maw has invited me to "come on over and haunt" her place on a permanent basis. "I guess a white lady ghost is better than no company at all," she said. "Anyway, it ain't like you got something more important to do for now." She's right, of course. But being dead with Maw-Maw around is a lot less boring than being dead all alone.

I tried to get Maw-Maw and Ashara to go get some counseling. We'd all been through something more than a little traumatic, and it seemed to me that they might feel better about it if they talked to a professional. But they both refused.

"I don't need to pay some fancy head doctor to tell me I got myself the post-traumatic stress. I know that already. But that's just what happens when bad times come around. I'll get to feeling better soon enough. Anyway, that old Howard boy can't hurt us none now." And that was the end of the conversation, as far as she was concerned.

When I brought the subject up with Ashara, she just shook her head. "No way," she said. "I ain't crazy."

So much for therapy.

The national news made a huge deal out of the fact that Molly was murdered by a couple of white supremacists. As if enough people aren't already convinced that most whites in the Deep South are racist. It's a shame, really, that only the bad stuff gets reported.

Ashara and Stephen are still doing just fine together, and stop by most nights for dinner. Turns out Stephen's quite the cook. I like to stand over the stove and let the smells wash over me. It's almost as good as eating.

Stephen tells us that Rick is doing about as well as could be expected. He's out of jail, but his family has been destroyed: his wife dead, his brother headed to prison for her murder. He sold the house he and Molly lived in together, but he's planning on staying in Abramsville and running his store, at least for the time being.

On other nights, the nights when Ashara and Stephen don't come by, Maw-Maw and I sometimes sit around and reminisce about our lives. We don't talk much about what happened to all of us out at the Howard place barn--I think we're still coming to terms with it all. I still think counseling is a good idea, but I've given up trying to convince Maw-Maw and Ashara and Stephen, for that matter. They're all just as stubborn as can be.

So, yeah. I'm pretty content with the way things are right now. Maw-Maw says she thinks this is probably some sort of temporary break for me. She thinks I've got more to do before I can move on to wherever it is that most people go when they die. The ones who don't wake up dead in Alabama.

"You mark my words, Callie Taylor," she's said on more than one occasion. "You ain't done here yet. You got more work to do, and when it comes, you'll know what it is."

I think she might be right, but I don't tell her that. Generally I answer with some version of "Nope. I'm stuck to you, so I'm just sitting here waiting for you to die so you can drag my bony white ass up to heaven."

Maw-Maw cackles at that, and we go back to watching television together.

We like the same crime shows.

The End

Acknowlegements

For all that there's a myth of the solitary writer—and writing a novel can, indeed, be a solitary act—publishing a book takes the efforts of many people, and I cannot express my gratitude enough for the people who have helped bring this book into the world.

First of all, I'd like to thank KateMarie Collins of Solstice Publishing for her patience as she guided me through this process.

Cyn Ley has been the best editor anyone could dream of; her comments and questions helped bring Callie to life. To all my social media contacts: thank you for your support!

Thanks also to the Solstice Publishing authors' group for encouragement and question-answering.

A special thanks to my online colleagues who brighten my day: Kamille, Nadine, and Melanie, the writing goes smoother because I can count on you to make my life more fun.

To Deborah Christie—there are not enough words to cover how lucky I feel to have you in my world.

To all the Taylors, from whom Callie took her surname: you are the family of my heart and my choosing, and I couldn't imagine my life without all of you in it.

To my family by blood and by marriage: thank you for your care and support; I love y'all!

My unending gratitude and love goes to my parents, Dan and Glenda Collins, for teaching me to cherish books and to follow my dreams—and for helping out with childcare as I finished this project!

And most of all, thanks go to my husband Elson for his steadfast generosity and love, even as I disappear into my writing, and to our darling daughter Isabel: this book is for you. I love you with all my heart.

~Margo Bond Collins
http://www.MargoBondCollins.com

Other Solstice Shadows Titles

A Pride of Lions
By
Mark Iles

When Selena Dillon is caught in an assassination attempt on her planet's ruler, she finds herself sentenced to twenty-five years servitude in the most feared military force, the Penal Regiments. Much to her surprise she enjoys the harsh military life and is quickly selected for officer training.

But something's wrong, worlds are falling silent. There's no cry for help and no warning, just a sudden eerie silence. When a flotilla of ships is despatched to investigate they exit hyperspace to find themselves facing a massive alien armada. Outnumbered and outgunned the flotilla fight a rearguard action, allowing one of their number to slip away and warn mankind.

As worlds fall in battle, and mankind's fleets are decimated, Selena is selected to lead a team of the Penal Regiment's most battle-hardened veterans, in a last ditch attempt to destroy the aliens' home world. If she fails mankind is doomed. Little does Selena know that one of her crew is a psychopathic killer and another is the husband of his victim. Can she hold her team together, get them to their target and succeed in the attack? Selena knows that if she fails then there will be nothing at all left to go home to.

An Element of Time
By
BeBe Knight

A vampire and a slayer walk into a bar… Sounds like
the beginning of a bad joke, but for Veronica and Mackenzie,
it's the beginning of the rest of their lives…

The world has seen its fair share of evil, but Veronica
Chase had no idea such monsters truly existed. Werewolves,
poltergeists, witches… even vampires. Ignorance was bliss.
But her reality was crushed on that horrid day her family was
taken away from her. Now, Veronica has devoted her entire
life to hunting those very creatures, searching for the werewolf
pack that murdered her parents in hopes of finding her
abducted sister. Nothing will get in her way of settling the
score for the hand she was unjustly dealt. That is until her
newest assignment brings her to her knees.
After one hundred and eight years on earth, Mackenzie
Jones thought he had seen it all. With the exception of daylight
of course, but that's what comes with the territory being a
vampire and all. Perpetually damned to live his life as a
bartender in the shadows of the night, nothing has sparked his
interest lately. Just once he wished something exciting would
happen in his mundane life. Little did he know, his wish was
about to come true. Walking through the door to his bar, and
into his heart, Mackenzie allows love to take the wheel for the
first time. There's just one slight problem. She's there to kill
him.

Mark of the Successor
By
KateMarie Collins

Dominated and controlled by an abusive mother, Lily does what she can to enjoy fleeting moments of normality. When a break from school only provides the opportunity for more abuse at home, the sudden appearance of a stranger turns her world even bleaker. Disappearing without a trace, he has left a lingering fear in Lily. His parting words to her mother, "Have her ready to travel tomorrow," is something her mind refuses to accept.

Running away is the only answer. But before Lily can execute her plan, a shimmering portal appears in her room. Along with two strangers who promise to help keep her safe. With time running out, she accepts their offer for escape and accompanies them into a brand new world. A world in which she is the kidnapped daughter of a Queen, and the heir to the throne of Tiadar.

Can she find her own strength to overcome both an abusive past and avoid those who would use her as a means to power?

A Zombie Romance
By
Chris Perdue

What if the zombies were the supernatural heroes
while the humans were the evil villains? What if the hero
Adam was a self-proclaimed dumbass who had only one
purpose in the world... to find his bad ass zombie girlfriend
Luna. And what if he found his beloved only to realize that she
had supernatural strength, was a hell of a lot smarter than him,
and was willing to use the lure of sexual gratification to bite
him? Yeah you get the idea... Adam is destined to become the
funniest zombie in history. Yet there are enigmas wrapped in
mysteries with riddles and other secretive juicy tidbits that lay
beneath the facade of the zombie condition. Stereotypical at
first, they evolve from their transitional state, and discover it is
their duty to save the world from humans. Just when you think
this book is over you realize the journey has just begun.

Made in the USA
San Bernardino, CA
29 March 2014